"You agree to be my mistress for one year, exclusively mine," he emphasized.

She understood, all right. One year in his bed; it was blackmail, pure and simple. Well, maybe not so pure…

"At the end of that time, I will give you the evidence of the fraud and cancel your debt," Marcus went on.

"I would prefer to pay back the money my *mother* stole." Eloise accented the word. "Not me," she added forcibly. She was not admitting a guilt she was not responsible for.

"That is not an option." But Marcus had to give her points for trying. She looked so defiant, her green eyes blazing, and infinitely desirable.

DI025454

GREEK TYCOONS

**They're the men who have everything—
except a bride...**

Wealth, power, charm—what else could a
heart-stoppingly handsome tycoon need?
In the GREEK TYCOONS miniseries you
have already been introduced to some
gorgeous Greek multimillionaires who are
in need of wives.

Now it's the turn of favorite
Presents® author **Jacqueline Baird**
with her passion-filled romance
THE GREEK TYCOON'S REVENGE.

Where Marcus Kouvaris demands that Eloise
become his mistress for a year...

Jacqueline Baird

THE GREEK TYCOON'S REVENGE

GREEK
TYCOONS

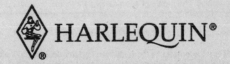

HARLEQUIN®

TORONTO • NEW YORK • LONDON
AMSTERDAM • PARIS • SYDNEY • HAMBURG
STOCKHOLM • ATHENS • TOKYO • MILAN • MADRID
PRAGUE • WARSAW • BUDAPEST • AUCKLAND

If you purchased this book without a cover you should be aware
that this book is stolen property. It was reported as "unsold and
destroyed" to the publisher, and neither the author nor the
publisher has received any payment for this "stripped book."

ISBN 0-373-12266-7

THE GREEK TYCOON'S REVENGE

First North American Publication 2002.

Copyright © 2002 by Jacqueline Baird.

All rights reserved. Except for use in any review, the reproduction or
utilization of this work in whole or in part in any form by any electronic,
mechanical or other means, now known or hereafter invented, including
xerography, photocopying and recording, or in any information storage
or retrieval system, is forbidden without the written permission of the
publisher, Harlequin Enterprises Limited, 225 Duncan Mill Road,
Don Mills, Ontario, Canada M3B 3K9.

All characters in this book have no existence outside the imagination of
the author and have no relation whatsoever to anyone bearing the same
name or names. They are not even distantly inspired by any individual
known or unknown to the author, and all incidents are pure invention.

This edition published by arrangement with Harlequin Books S.A.

® and TM are trademarks of the publisher. Trademarks indicated with
® are registered in the United States Patent and Trademark Office, the
Canadian Trade Marks Office and in other countries.

Visit us at www.eHarlequin.com

Printed in U.S.A.

CHAPTER ONE

'I'M NOT even going to get to first base, am I, honey?'

Eloise's luscious lips parted over even white teeth in a stunning smile, her green eyes sparkling with amusement. 'No, Ted. You're not.' She shook her head, her red-gold hair swaying gently around her slender shoulders, and not being able to stop herself, she laughed out loud at the exaggerated woebegone expression on her companion's face.

'I knew it. When your luck is out, it's out,' Ted Charlton stated in his deep American drawl. 'But what the hell? Eloise you're a great companion, and we can still talk— more than I could ever do with my ex-wife, that's for sure.'

Ted had told her over the meal that he was in the process of getting divorced for the third time as his wife had run off with a younger man, and Eloise felt sorry for him. Probably about fifty, he was no Adonis, but his personality and wit more than made up for his homely appearance.

'*You* certainly can,' Eloise teased him. 'I think I know your life story from high school.'

'Heaven forbid—I am boring you.'

Bravely she reached out and placed her hand on his arm. 'No truly, you've led such a fascinating life. I hope I have even half as much fun.'

'A beautiful talented girl like you, the world is your oyster. It gives the old ego a boost simply to be seen out with you, and if I can help you in any way I can, I will.'

It wasn't a cast-iron contract to invest in KHE, the jewellery design company she shared with her two friends,

Katy and her husband Harry, but it was almost as good as, Eloise thought happily.

'That's very kind of you.' She beamed at her companion. She had never dined with a prospective investor in her life, and she would not have been doing it now, except Katy—who was seven and a half months pregnant—had not been feeling well. Harry, who looked after the business side of things, wanted to stay at home with his wife, but had arranged a dinner with Ted Charlton, and so Eloise had been railroaded into taking his place.

'Not kind; it's just common sense. You and your friends really have something; in a few years I can see KHE jewellery boutiques in every capital in the world.'

Eloise laughed out loud. 'Now you're exaggerating.' She was glad she had taken Harry's place; the evening was a success and the relief was enormous, both business-wise and personally...

She hadn't wanted to come. Dinner dates and dancing were not her scene. The flimsy top she was wearing was not hers, but Katy's. Eloise's preference was for casual trousers and baggy shirts, but surprisingly Ted Charlton had somehow put her at her ease, and she was amazed to realise she was actually enjoying herself.

'Maybe,' Ted said, rising to his feet. 'But how about you to take a chance on my old bones and dance with me? We can leave the business details until tomorrow, with your astute Harry around to dot the i's and cross the t's.'

For a split second she hesitated; then, rising to her feet, Eloise took his outstretched hand. 'Sure thing, Ted,' she said in an appalling attempt at an American accent and they were both laughing as they moved around the small dance floor in each other's arms.

* * *

Marcus Kouvaris leant back against the bar, a glass of whisky in his hand, and slid his other hand into the pocket of his trousers. The stunningly attractive blonde at his side immediately slipped her arm through his, allowing her small breasts to press against him. He flicked her a knowing, sensuous smile. They both knew where the evening would end—in bed... Nadine was a top model and a more experienced sexual athlete he had yet to meet: and he needed the relief. Marcus took a sip of his whisky and frowned.

He'd spent a great deal of the past twelve months at his villa on the Greek island of Rykos, keeping a protective eye on his Aunt Christine, his late mother's sister, and her daughter Stella, who had their permanent home there. He'd been trying to give them the comfort and support they needed after the tragic death of their husband and father, Theo Toumbis, in a car crash. Unfortunately it had seriously curtailed his sex life, and celibacy was not his style.

He was in London for a few days on private business. But he intended to bed the very willing Nadine every night, though he was far too wary a male to let her know that. Marcus took another swallow of the amber nectar, glanced idly around the room, and stilled.

It could have been a couple of frozen peas rubbing against his arm for all the effect Nadine's breasts had on him. His teeth clenched and his dark eyes narrowed in angry recognition on the couple seated at the table on the other side of the dance floor. The man he dismissed with a fleeting glance. But the female...the female was Eloise...innocent, virginal Eloise, who blushed when a man so much as looked at her!

As Marcus watched, he saw the girl lean forward and place a hand on the much older man's arm, and smile up at her companion.

Marcus's firm lips curved in a hard cynical smile; it

confirmed what his informant had told him. Eloise was certainly her *mother's* daughter...the mother who had conned his Uncle Theo out of a great deal of money with Eloise's assistance. The reason Marcus was in London was to gain recompense for his aunt and cousin.

The money was not important to him with his wealth; supporting his aunt and cousin didn't even dent his finances. But it was a matter of principle. Nobody stole from him or his family and walked away free.

On a more personal level he harboured a nagging doubt that Eloise had played him for a sucker with her professed virginity. He'd respected her innocence and restrained himself to some light kisses the last time they met, only to have her disappear without a word. Nobody made a fool of Marcus Kouvaris and got away with it...

His dark eyes narrowed on the object of his thoughts. Eloise, if anything, was even more beautiful than she had been at nineteen, and when she rose to her feet his dark eyes trailed over her in a blatant male appreciation. Her upper body was clad in a gold camisole that revealed the creamy mounds of her breasts, before slipping into the waistband of a long black crepe skirt, demure in its slightly flared style until she moved. Then an enticing length of leg was exposed by the subtle slit in one side. A gold belt heightened the whole elegant effect, emphasising her tiny waist, and three-inch gold sandals completed the picture.

He felt an instant stirring in his groin and it had nothing to do with the woman he was with. His dark eyes narrowed angrily. Dammit! But Eloise was some woman. The epitome of femininity, she moved with an instinctive grace, and when she smiled her incredible green eyes glowed, and further highlighted the pale, almost translucent skin that contrasted so stunningly with the fiery red hair.

Five years! Instinctively the hand in his pocket curved

into a fist, his fingers tingling. He could remember as if it were yesterday the silken softness of her skin, the feel of her in his arms, and his body hardened further. He tore his gaze away from Eloise and looked at her companion. He recognised the man from the financial papers. Ted Charlton, a wealthy American entrepreneur who had recently parted from his wife.

A thunderous frown creased his smooth brow. Marcus had intended giving Eloise the benefit of the doubt; she had been very young and probably under her mother's influence. The report lying on the desk in his penthouse suite stated that KHE was a small but successful jewellery design company with a lot of potential. Reading it, Marcus had no doubt KHE was the same company his Uncle Theo had thought he was investing in, Eloise by Design. It was the same business plan and one of the same partners that had signed the contract with Theo five years ago. Eloise Baker! Even so, Marcus had been prepared to negotiate the repayment of Theo's investment from profits in a businesslike manner. But seeing Eloise dancing and laughing with the older man filled him with such fury, he changed his mind.

Marcus Kouvaris had never suffered from jealousy in his life and consequently did not recognise the emotion. But suddenly he was wishing he hadn't dismissed the investigator he had hired to find Eloise quite so finally over the telephone. The man had called him in Greece a couple of weeks ago, and said he had found Eloise, who turned out not to be Chloe's sister, but her daughter. He'd given Eloise's address in London and the name of her company. Marcus had asked if Eloise was guilty of any other frauds, and the detective had drawled she was as pure as the driven snow, with a rather nasty laugh at the end of it.

When the detective had asked if he should forward the

personal file he had on Eloise, Marcus had told him to bin it. He only needed Eloise's address. He couldn't admit even to himself, he didn't like the idea of reading a list of her lovers.

Now he decided it was time to do some investigation of his own into the elegant Eloise, and he smiled with malice as he watched the pair.

Held comfortably in the arms of her companion, Eloise glanced around. The supper club, in the heart of London's Mayfair, was the latest in place to dine. The food and service were superb, the lighting discreet, the women beautiful, and the men wealthy. She gave a contented sigh as Ted led her expertly around the small dance floor. She had conquered a personal fear, and unless she was very much mistaken Ted Charlton was going to invest in their company.

'Don't look now,' Ted said softly, close to her ear. 'But there's a man standing by the bar who's been watching you like a hawk for the past few minutes, and is now looking daggers at me.'

Of course Eloise did look. Immediately her green eyes clashed across the crowded room with narrowed black. For a long moment she was incapable of looking away. Her heart made a crazy leap in her chest. 'Oh,' she gasped, and stumbled.

Marcus tilted his arrogant head back, and arched one perfectly formed brow apparently in query, then slowly allowed his gaze to roam over her slender body with studied masculine appraisal, before returning to her face, his eyes widening in supposedly surprised recognition. His expressive features relaxed; a slow sensual smile parted his firm lips as he lifted his glass towards Eloise in acknowledgement of her presence.

Ted's arm tightened protectively around her waist, just as the music stopped. 'You know him?' he asked as he turned her away from the stranger and led her back to the table.

'You could say that.' Eloise picked up her champagne glass, with a hand that shook, and drained it before replacing it on the table. She tried to smile but her composure had taken a heck of a jolt. 'I met him in Greece on holiday years ago, but I haven't seen him since.'

'A holiday romance?' Ted prompted.

'Yes.' She sighed. 'I suppose it was.' She hadn't thought so at the time. She'd thought he was the love of her life. He was the first man Eloise had ever had a crush on—the only man, she silently admitted. They had met thrice, and then he had to leave suddenly to visit his ailing father, and she'd returned to England, and had never heard from him again. Perhaps it was just as well, as when her mother had explained Marcus Kouvaris was a financial wizard who had made a fortune from the technology boom and, unlike some, had hung on to it, and made more, Eloise knew he was well out of her reach.

'Eloise. It is Eloise Baker?' The deep, slightly accented voice was instantly recognisable, and slowly she lifted her head.

Eloise could feel the colour rise in her cheeks as involuntarily her green eyes flickered over his tall, broad-shouldered frame. Older, but he was still as incredibly attractive as ever. Thick black hair, olive-toned skin, with perfectly symmetrical features, a firm jaw and a smile guaranteed to make any woman melt...

'Eloise, yes,' she confirmed with a tentative smile. 'But Smith, not Baker,' she corrected him without thinking. At least he had remembered her first name, if not her second;

that was some consolation given he was notorious for the number of women he dated.

'Smith, of course, but it has been a long time,' Marcus said smoothly. Without realising it Eloise had admitted she'd lied. His gaze swept over her, her eyes were the green of the finest emeralds. Her cheeks were streaked with a becoming shade of pink, innocence personified.

Marcus's belly knotted. He couldn't recall ever being this angry with anyone in his life, and it took all his formidable willpower to stop himself dragging her by the glorious red hair from her seat and throttling her with it. But instead, using all his considerable charm, he added, 'Though you don't look a day older, and if it is possible even more beautiful than you were at nineteen.'

Eloise could feel her face burning even brighter at his open flattery. 'Thank-you,' she mumbled and, tearing her gaze away from his dark compelling eyes, she finally noticed the blonde hanging on his arm.

'Allow me to introduce my friend,' Marcus said coolly, catching the direction of her gaze. 'Nadine, this is Eloise, an old friend of mine, and her companion...' Marcus turned his attention to the older man watching the exchange with astute blue eyes. 'Ted Charlton, I believe. We haven't been introduced but—' and he mentioned some financial article, and the two men shook hands.

Eloise took the slender limp hand Nadine offered her, and wasn't surprised at the other woman's cold smile. If Eloise had been on a date with Marcus, she would not have wanted company either. She could still remember how he had affected her five years ago and how heartbroken she had been when her mother insisted they had to leave the villa on Rykos before Marcus had returned to the island.

Eloise had left a note with her address in England for

Marcus with the maid. She had lived in hope for over a year that he would contact her again, but then circumstances changed her attitude and she stopped wondering and waiting for him; she had bigger things to worry about.

'Join us for a drink.' Ted made the conventional offer.

'Some other time, perhaps,' Nadine cut in before Marcus could speak and, linking her arm firmly through the tall Greek's, she smiled. 'Your friends have already eaten, Marcus, and I am starving. You did promise me dinner.' She pouted, her long red fingernails stroking down the sleeve of his jacket. 'For starters,' she purred.

Eloise suppressed a grimace of distaste at Nadine's obvious seduction technique.

'Nadine, darling, I'm sure you can wait a while.' He smiled at his girlfriend, but the tone of his voice warned her not to argue.

Seats were pulled out and another bottle of champagne ordered.

'To old friends.' Marcus raised his glass and looked directly at Eloise. Her eyes met and fused with his and for a moment she was transported back in time to a Greek island, and her heart raced again as it had then, the first time they'd met.

'And hopefully new ones,' Marcus continued, addressing Ted.

They all touched glasses, and Eloise took a hasty swallow of the sparkling liquid. She was shocked at the rush of awareness simply being in Marcus's company had aroused in her. She had thought herself over him long ago, and she was grateful for Nadine's timely contribution to the sudden silence.

'Marcus and I have known each other for almost two years and he has never mentioned you. So when did you meet him?' Nadine demanded, her gimlet eyes fixed on Eloise.

'I was on holiday with my m…sister, Chloe,' she stammered, feeling the colour rise in her face. 'We had rented a villa on the island of Rykos in Greece. Chloe was a friend of Marcus's Uncle Theo, who was the developer and had built the villa along with five others. When we held a pool party Theo brought Marcus along to the party and we…'

Marcus almost snorted in disgust. 'How is your sister?' he cut in abruptly. The detective he had hired had taken almost a year to unravel Chloe Baker's various names, before discovering the woman had never had a sister but a daughter with the name of Smith. Probably the most common surname in the English language…

Eloise glanced across the table at Marcus. Hooded dark eyes hard as steel stared back at her. Did he know she'd lied all those years ago? But her mother had insisted she called her Chloe, and pretend to be sisters. At thirty-six, Chloe was not going to admit to having a grown-up daughter, and Eloise had agreed. Or was he frightened she would tell his girlfriend all the details of their brief romance? He must really care for Nadine.

'My sister died over three years ago,' Eloise mumbled. She hated lying, and suddenly realised there was no need to any more—her mother was dead. But now was not the time or the place.

'I am sorry.' Marcus mouthed the polite response but there was a singularly lack of sympathy in his expression. 'Chloe was a quite remarkable woman.'

She was, Eloise thought sadly, and if it had not been for her mother, she would never have been able to set up in business herself, but she had never really got to know her mother well. Pregnant at seventeen by a sailor, Tom

Smith, Chloe had married him, and divorced him three months after Eloise was born. Then she had left Eloise with her grandparents to be brought up in the small Northumberland coastal town of Alnmouth and disappeared. Four years later she returned with a different name after another failed marriage, loaded down with presents for her little girl, and apparently had become a very successful businesswoman. From then on she popped in every year or so…

For Eloise her mother had been a fairytale figure, beautiful and elegant in designer clothes, bringing gifts. It was only after the death of her grandparents, when she had completed her first year in art college, that her mother had actually spent some time with her. Chloe had taken a real interest in what Eloise was doing and declared herself fascinated by her daughter's skilful designs, and even suggested they go on holiday to Greece and so they had taken their first and last holiday together on Rykos.

'Sorry, I have brought back sad memories.' Marcus rose from the table and held out his hand to Eloise. 'Come dance with me and blow away the cobwebs of the past.'

'But—' Nadine said sharply.

'Then, Nadine, we will eat, I promise.' He shot his girlfriend a brilliant smile, and a brief glance at Ted. 'With your permission, of course, old man?' he asked while clasping Eloise's hand and urging her to her feet, not waiting for an answer.

'Nadine is going to die of hunger if you don't feed her soon,' Eloise tried to joke, as Marcus slipped an arm around her waist and pulled her firmly against the long powerful length of his body.

He was taller than she remembered; she had to tilt her head back to look up at him, but that was a mistake. The years had been kind to him, and close up he was even more staggeringly handsome than she remembered. An aggressively virile, sophisticated male, he exuded an aura of raw sexuality that the formal tailored dinner suit and white silk shirt did nothing to hide, and it terrified her.

'Nadine's hunger is never for food,' he returned, a mockingly sensual smile curving his wide mouth. 'She is a model; she doesn't eat enough to feed a bird. You, on the other hand, are every man's fantasy of the female form.' His hand at her back slowly stroked up her spine and just as slowly down to settle rather low on her bottom, while his other hand clasped hers and held it firmly against his broad chest.

'Are you implying I'm fat?' she said with mock horror, fighting to appear the sophisticated woman when inside she was quaking.

Marcus let his gaze drop to the firm thrust of her obviously braless breasts against the gold fabric, and then back to her face. 'God forbid! You have the perfect figure. Full and fat are not the same thing.' And the hand he had held firm against his chest somehow contrived to be held against hers, his knuckles brushing against the soft upper swell of her breast.

She should have been horrified. She had never been this close to a man in four years, never wanted to be. But now, to her utter amazement, she felt her nipples harden against the fine silk of her top, and she had to drop her eyes to his chest to mask the sudden flare of desire that heated her face. A tiny pulse at the base of her throat was racing, and she was appalled yet secretly thrilled by her helpless response to his innately sensual masculinity.

'I do believe you are blushing, Eloise,' Marcus teased as he moved her expertly around the floor to the sexy soft tones of a well-known Barry White recording.

'It's hot in here.' She made herself look up at him.

Marcus's perceptive black eyes ran over her now scarlet face, and deliberately he tightened his arm around her, bringing her into impossibly close contact with his long, lean length. He felt the tremor in her body, and he fought to mask the cynical smile of masculine satisfaction that threatened his oh, so caring features, even as he fought to mask his own body's instant arousal. He dipped his head and whispered softly in her ear, 'And getting hotter by the minute.'

He was flirting with her, Eloise knew, and she should have been angry, but the reverse was true. The slender fingers of her hand flexed, curved into his broad shoulder, and clung. His warm breath, his hard body, the softly murmured words all conspired to turn Eloise's bones to mush; her legs felt wobbly, and her heart felt as if it would burst. It was as if the trauma of the past had been swept away and once again she was the adolescent teenager, totally besotted by the sophisticated overpowering charm of Marcus Kouvaris.

'Your girlfriend,' Eloise got out. What was Marcus trying to do to her? And in the middle of the dance floor with Nadine watching. 'Nadine,' she choked.

'Forget Nadine. I did, the moment I saw you again,' Marcus declared throatily, and observed the deepening colour in her cheeks with a cynical cool. God! The woman could blush on demand, but nothing of his thoughts showed on his chiselled features as his gaze roamed over the perfect oval of her face. 'Why did you leave me without a word, Eloise?' he asked softly, his dark eyes looking soulfully down into hers.

'But I thought you left me.' In shock at her own reactions, she answered honestly. 'I waited ten days for you to contact me. Then we had to leave.' She hadn't wanted to, but her mother had insisted. 'But I left you a note with my address and telephone number with the maid.'

'My father died from the heart attack, and by the time the funeral was over it was two weeks before I could return to the villa. It was empty, no sign of a maid or a letter.'

'I'm sorry about your father.' Eloise's green eyes shaded with compassion.

'Yes, well, it was a few years ago now.' He shrugged his broad shoulders. 'But I definitely never received a note from you, Eloise, believe me.'

With his hand stroking her back, and his expression sincere, she believed him. 'I do. These things happen,' she mumbled.

'I guess the time wasn't right for us then.' He squeezed her gently and her pulse rate went into overdrive. 'But the past is past and I am delighted to have met you again. I often wondered what happened to you,' he said smoothly.

Wondered? Some understatement; a bitter smile tightened Marcus's mouth. When he'd returned to the island and found her gone, he'd ruefully conceded she was the one that got away and tried to dismiss her from his mind. He didn't chase after women, they chased after him, but she had haunted his dreams for years. It was only after Theo's death and he was left with settling the man's affairs that he had hired someone to find her *sister* Chloe, and only recently he had discovered Eloise Smith was the daughter, not the sister, of the devious late Chloe Baker. Seeing her with Ted had finally cured him of the romantic picture he'd carried in his head of an innocent young girl forced by her wicked mother into fraud! The gods must be laughing, he thought irreverently. But he allowed none of his thoughts to show. He eased her slightly away from him.

'I would love to see you again and catch up with what

you are doing.' He gazed down into her beautiful face. 'Have dinner with me tomorrow night?' He held her closer, one long leg easing between hers, as he moved her skilfully in a turn. 'Please.' He watched the green eyes widen with a mixture of fear and excitement, and almost laughed out loud. She had good reason to fear him, the devious little witch—but her sort could never resist a challenge, he knew; he'd met enough in his time.

'Will your girlfriend mind?' The friction of his hard thigh against hers, even through the thickness of their clothes, was enough to send every nerve in her body haywire and Eloise said the first thing that entered her bemused brain.

'Not at all. Nadine and I understand each other; we are casual friends, nothing more.' And, easing her slightly away from him, he added, 'But I'm forgetting your boyfriend, Ted.' This time, Marcus could not keep the hard edge of cynicism out of his tone. 'Will he object to you dating another man?'

Eased from the close contact with his lithe body, Eloise did not know whether to be relieved or aggrieved. He aroused a host of sensations she had never thought she would experience again and she wasn't sure she wanted to. Relief won.

'You're kidding.' She chuckled. 'Ted is a charming man but he isn't my boyfriend. Tonight is a business dinner, nothing more.' That Marcus could imagine even for a moment that she would go out with a man old enough to be her father was ludicrous, and consequently she told him the truth.

'In that case, give me your telephone number.' His eyes narrowed on her laughing face and his large body tensed as he let her go. Was she up to her late mother's tricks, and so sure of success that she had readily admitted her involvement with Ted Charlton was simply business? Marcus needed to know more, but this wasn't the right time to question her, with Nadine waiting at the table for him and Ted watching Eloise like a drooling fool.

Eloise felt the sudden tension in his body, just before his arm fell from her waist; her puzzled gaze shot to his but his expression was bland. Then she realised it was because the music had stopped.

'Your number, Eloise?' Marcus murmured as, with one hand lightly in the centre of her back, he urged her towards the table.

Still in a state of shock at the unexpected meeting and her own response to Marcus, Eloise reeled off her number. 'You will never remember it,' and added, 'but our company, KHE, designer jewellery, is in the directory.'

She did not see his strong handsome face harden into disgust at the mention of designer jewellery, or the flare of white-hot fury in his dark eyes, as he stood behind her and pulled out her chair. By the time she was seated and she had recovered some slight control over her racing pulse and scattered nerves enough to join in the general conversation, and finally look at Marcus, he was all urbane charm and about to leave with Nadine.

'A very impressive man,' Ted said as Eloise watched Marcus and Nadine stroll off to where their table awaited them. The maître d' stood hovering around the pair like a mother hen. But then, a man of Marcus Kouvaris's power and wealth commanded that kind of attention wherever he went, Eloise thought wryly.

'Yes, Ted.' She sighed and turned her attention back to Ted. 'Nadine is a lucky woman.'

'No, you're wrong there, Eloise. She hasn't a hope in hell of catching Kouvaris. But you—you watch out. Take it from a man who knows his own sex. I saw the way

Kouvaris looked, and danced with you. But I have heard rumours about his womanising, and you are far too nice a lady for a man of his reputation.'

'I'll take that as a compliment,' Eloise said softly. 'But I don't think you need worry.' And, with a swift glance at the other couple, the black head touching the blonde, she grinned ruefully back at Ted. 'You're right, he's way out of my league.'

They finished off their dinner with coffee, and Ted persuaded Eloise to make a night of it, so they stayed to watch the late-night cabaret, and dance. It was a fun evening, and Eloise was yawning widely by the time Ted took her home in a taxi.

At the door of the town house where Eloise lived and worked, Ted smiled teasingly down at her. 'I won't come in, before you ask, but thank you for a lovely evening, Eloise, and you can tell your partners they have nothing to worry about. I will invest. I'll be in touch with Harry in the morning to do the deal. Okay?' Planting a brief kiss on her cheek, he said, 'Good night.'

Letting herself into the elegant entrance hall, Eloise ran lightly up the staircase, and stopped at the first floor. She glanced at her wristwatch, and grimaced. Three a.m. It was far too late to call on Katy and Harry now and tell them the good news and she turned to mount the next flight of stairs.

Strictly speaking, the house was Eloise's, but it was also the biggest asset of the company. The basement was the work room, the ground floor the showroom and offices, the first floor was Katy and Harry's apartment, the second floor Eloise's, and the attic apartment was rented by a gay couple.

Julian and Jeff were two beautiful young men. Julian earned his living as a freelance photographer and had made up a fantastic catalogue for KHE jewellery, and also talked quite a few models into wearing it, and that had been instrumental in getting the firm noticed and into several of the glossy magazines. Jeff worked in the showroom of KHE and was great at selling. The female customers adored him, and the male customers, while taking his advice, were not threatened by his beauty. For Eloise it was the ideal set-up; she loved the house and felt perfectly safe.

'Is that you, Eloise?' A stage whisper broke into Eloise's thoughts and, swinging around, she ran lightly back down the stairs and straight into the arms of Harry.

'Break out the champagne, folks. Ted is going to come in with us,' she said as Harry swung her around and into the open door of their apartment where Katy was waiting looking, thankfully, very well, if rather round.

'You're sure?' Katy grasped her arm and pulled her into the sitting room. 'Tell all.'

Half an hour later her two friends had the whole story.

'So…' Katy looked mischievous but beautiful with her black curly hair and big brown eyes; she fixed Eloise with a speculative glance. 'We can take it the business will expand, much like my waistline. But what about this Mr Kouvaris? Wasn't that the name of the chap you met, and then left you on that holiday with your mother?'

Immediately on the defensive, Eloise said, 'Marcus didn't leave me—he was called away because his father was ill, and apparently the old man died.' It was strange to be saying his name out loud after five years of trying to forget it, and stupidly she could feel herself blushing. 'It was no big deal and look, it's four o'clock in the morning. We'll talk tomorrow.'

She was still trying to convince herself of the fact ages

later lying in her queen-sized bed, unable to sleep. She did not want to take a sleeping tablet the doctor had prescribed. She hadn't used them in years, and simply seeing Marcus Kouvaris again was not going to drive her into taking one.

CHAPTER TWO

INSTEAD she practised her relaxation exercises, turned on her back, and let her mind roam freely back to her holiday in Greece.

Eloise had been carrying a tray of drinks out on to the terrace when she had first seen Marcus. He was standing next to her mother and Theo Toumbis by the edge of the swimming pool, laughing at something her mother had said. Eloise had nearly dropped the tray, such was the instant effect of his sheer male beauty on her teenage heart. Dressed casually in white shorts, and a shirt open down the front revealing his muscular chest with a sprinkling of black body hair, and long legs glazed in gold by the afternoon sun, the man looked like the reincarnation of a Greek god to Eloise's naïve eyes and she had stood transfixed simply staring at him.

'Stop loitering, *sis*, we are dying of thirst here.' Her mother's command had the ten or so people around the pool turning to look at her, including Marcus.

Eloise blushed scarlet, and for a second Marcus's eyes met hers, before she dropped her head and stepped forward.

Miraculously he appeared at her side. 'Here, let me take that. A beautiful young girl like you should be waited on, not the other way around.' And that was how it had started...

He'd introduced himself as Theo's nephew and had encouraged her to strip off the long cotton shift that concealed her white skinned, bikini-clad body, and join him

in the pool. Marcus in his swimming trunks was enough
to make any woman weak at the knees, and Eloise had
been no exception. He had talked and teased and flirted
with her and by the end of the evening he knew she was
an unattached nineteen-year-old student on holiday abroad
for the first time in her life with her sister Chloe who had
rented the villa.

Eloise had hated lying to him, but her mother had insisted no one should know they were mother and daughter,
and it had seemed a small price to pay to spend time with
her mother. Eloise knew her mother loved her in her own
way; she had proved it when after the funeral of her parents Chloe had not even minded that they had left all they
owned to Eloise, including the house. Eloise had felt terrible, and it had taken all her powers of persuasion to get
her mum to at least take the money from the sale of the
house. Even so her mum suggested she set up a joint account and they could share the proceeds. Eloise happily
agreed, but never touched the account until after her
mother's death.

Stirring restlessly on the bed, Eloise ran the tip of her
tongue over her full lips; it seemed like only yesterday she
had felt the touch of Marcus's lips on hers for the first
time. Sighing, she rolled over on her stomach and buried
her head in the pillow, the memories coming thick and
fast.

Before Marcus had finally left, well after midnight, he'd
gathered Eloise gently into his arms and kissed her, and
from that moment she knew she was in love.

At ten the next morning Marcus had turned up in an
open-topped sports car, and whisked her away to the other
side of the island.

'Come on, sweetheart.' Marcus stopped the car only a
few feet away from the edge of a cliff, stepped out and

was holding open the passenger door with one hand and a picnic basket in the other with a blanket over his arm. 'We're going to have a picnic.'

'Here?' Eloise glanced around the rocky outcrop not more that a yard square.

'Trust me.' Marcus grinned, and she did.

The steps were cut deep into an almost vertical cliff, with an old rope strung along the cliff face as a handrail. It was the scariest walk Eloise had ever experienced in her young life, and when she finally stepped onto the smooth sand at the base of the cliff her legs were trembling. Marcus dropped the hamper and the blanket on the white sand and gathered her into his arms.

'All right?'

Fighting to steady her erratic breathing, whether it was from the descent or the sensation of being enfolded against his hard, lean, scantily-clad body, she did not know, Eloise looked around and then up into his grinning face. 'It's perfect.' It was a totally secluded horseshoe shape of sand that led down to sparkling blue sea.

After a swim, they shared a meal of cold meat, chicken, salad, and fresh crusty bread, washed down with champagne.

'You're spoiling me.' Eloise sighed, lying back on the blanket, replete and perfectly happy.

Propped up on one elbow, Marcus's dark eyes sparkled with amusement and something more as they met hers. Suddenly the clear summer air shimmered with tension. 'This is nothing to what I would like to do for you,' he murmured huskily, the index finger of one hand gently outlining her lips. 'For your mouth,' he husked; the finger trailed down her throat, and lingered for a moment on the pulse beating madly there. 'For your elegant neck,' and then lower to the valley between her breasts. 'For your luscious breasts.' His voice thickened.

Eloise felt as though she was touched by fire, every nerve-end in her body tingling with vibrant life. She linked her hands around his neck, her fingers tangling in the silky black hair of his head. Marcus raised his head and moved so he was straddling her trembling body, and then gently brought his mouth down on hers, the tip of his tongue outlining her lips and, as her mouth opened, plunging deep into the moist sweet depths. Electric excitement thrilled through her, the rub of his thighs against the outside of her hips incredibly erotic, and as his mouth followed the path his finger had so recently taken, her excitement built higher and higher.

He buried his head in the valley between her breasts, and somehow her bikini top was no more. She trembled violently as he murmured something huskily in Greek, before his tongue licked across the crown of her breast, and very gently suckled the rosy tip in his mouth.

A lightning flare of response struck her without warning, and her body arched up against his hard, lean frame, brushing his groin in helpless response.

Marcus lifted his head, and gazed down into her dazed green eyes. 'You like that,' he husked. With one hand he stroked down from her breast to the tiny waist to lay flat on her belly. 'Tell me what more you like, my Eloise?' he demanded throatily, while his mouth found her other breast and repeated the sensual assault.

Eloise had never experienced anything like it before, yet somehow it all seemed natural—Marcus, the kiss, his touch. Tremor after tremor coursed through her veins as his other hand swept down the length of her body, from hips to thigh to calf and back up. His touch scorched her sensitive skin like a brand, and her breasts ached with a pleasure that she did not know existed, creating a need for more and more of the miraculous sensations.

His long fingers effortlessly slipped under the last scrap of material covering her nakedness, and suddenly Eloise tensed in innocent fear of where her wild emotions were leading. Her hands fell to push against his chest. 'No, no.' He was going too far, too fast…

Marcus jerked his head back, and her hands dropped to her sides. 'No. You say "No," but you want me.' His keen gaze raked the full length of her near-naked body, the pointed tips of her breasts, and then back to her eyes.

She stared up at him, her lips parted to speak. She did want him, but… Her green eyes huge, she glanced past him to the sea.

'You're not a tease, I hope?' his deep voice demanded hardily and she glanced back at him. 'I abhor women who lead a man on, lie with their body.'

'No. No.' Eloise could not bear him to look at her so cynically. 'It's just, I… Well, I haven't.' She could feel her skin getting even hotter but it was not with excitement, it was with embarrassment. He was a twenty-nine-year-old sophisticated man of the world; how could she tell him…? 'I've never, I haven't—' She lowered her lashes over her too revealing eyes, and swallowed hard. 'I'm a virgin.'

'A virgin?' he exclaimed. 'You're not protected.' His black eyes widened in stunned amazement, and then narrowed at her guileless face, the blush that suffused her skin, and a slow smile parted his sensual mouth. 'Ah,' he murmured and from that moment on his whole attitude changed.

Marcus was transformed from a sophisticated sensual male on the make, into a tender, caring companion. The rest of the day he treated her like some rare species of the female sex, though he could not stop touching her. But his touch was light on her silken skin, the few kisses they shared undemanding. When they parted later that night with a promise to meet again the next day, the kiss he pressed on her soft lips started as a gentle good night and quickly developed into a passionate embrace. But with iron self-control he ended it with a curse in Greek and a softly mouthed promise. 'I am going to make everything perfect for you, Eloise.'

Eloise went to bed that night with a head full of dreams of love and marriage, and the next morning Marcus arrived and told her his father was ill, he had to leave, she had been sad, but not unduly worried, as he'd promised to return.

Yawning wildly, Eloise rolled over onto her side and burrowing deeper under the duvet. March in England was cold. Not like Greece, she thought wryly. But then her Greek dream had ended long ago and she would do better to forget the memories, and get on with her life today. She would go out to dinner with Marcus for old times' sake, but that was all it would be, all it could be, now...

'We've done it, girls.' Harry came dashing into the basement workroom, with Jeff hot on his heels, waving a bottle of champagne, and a grinning Ted Charlton bringing up the rear.

Eloise looked up from her drawing board and Katy put the soldering tool down carefully on the workbench and slowly stood up, her eyes flicking from Harry to the older man.

'You're sure, Mr Charlton? Aren't you supposed to be looking after the showroom, Jeff?' she said sternly, but her brown eyes were alight with excitement.

'I'm sure, lady.' Ted chuckled. 'So sure I have per-

suaded your husband and Jeff here to close the showroom
and let me take everyone out to lunch to celebrate.'

Eloise said nothing but the grin on her face said it all.

Five minutes later, the bottle of champagne was opened
and the five all raised their glasses. 'To KHE, Paris.
Thanks to you, Ted.' Harry made the toast.

Over lunch the deal was discussed. The money Ted was
investing would be used for the creation of a KHE boutique in Paris. Better still, Ted actually knew of a property
for lease on the Rue St Honoré, one of the most fashion-
able streets in Paris, and he reckoned if Harry got in quick
it could be theirs. Harry had already made the booking for
his flight to France the next day and a meeting with the
owners, and he had the cheque for the first instalment of
Ted's financing in his pocket.

The entry phone rang, and Eloise cast a last hasty look at
her reflection in the mirrored door of the wardrobe. She
grimaced slightly. She had tried for the sophisticated look,
and had swept up her hair in a French pleat, and apart
from the black skirt she had worn last night, she was wearing the only thing she possessed that was not casual: the
suit she had bought for Katy's wedding. A fine wool jade
green suit in a classic style, the jacket short and with a
matching camisole underneath, the straight skirt ending an
inch above her knees, and kitten-heeled black pumps on
her feet. Conservative, she told herself, except for the intricately set silver and amber pendant around her neck and
the matching amber earrings, both her own designs.

Katy had been right last night when she'd made Eloise
borrow the gold camisole. It was way past time Eloise
updated her wardrobe. But, working behind the scenes in
the jewellery business designing and manufacturing, her
wardrobe consisted of jeans and sweaters, and a few vo-

luminous Indian cotton caftans, for when the weather was hot. But it was too late to worry about the state of her wardrobe now and, snatching up her purse, she dashed from the bedroom through to the sitting room to the door of her apartment, just as someone knocked on the door.

Surprised for a second, she hesitated and the knock sounded again, and she opened the door.

Marcus was leaning negligently against the doorframe, wearing a superbly elegant dark blue suit, and looking every inch the incredibly attractive, sophisticated male of her dreams.

Heat prickled her skin. 'How did you get in?' she demanded. It was not the opening she had planned, it sounded rather aggressive even to her own ears.

'Hello to you, too.' A sardonic brow arched. 'Shall I go out and start again.'

'N-no, of course not.' Eloise stammered, badly shaken by her instant response to his powerful presence.

'Relax, Eloise, your friend Harry downstairs opened the front door.' He smiled.

His smile dazzled her and, with his hand at her elbow supporting her, Eloise felt vaguely protected and actually did manage to relax slightly. 'Harry and Katy are my business partners,' she offered.

'He sounded more like your guardian.' Marcus remarked with a wry twist of his lips. 'He managed, in the space of less than a minute, to ask me who I was, where I was taking you, and what time I intended bringing you back.'

'That sounds like Harry,' Eloise confirmed with a chuckle, as they exited the outer door to the street. 'Katy and I met him when we were at art college and looking for somewhere to live. He managed the estate agents, and he took one look at Katy and fell in love. He found us an apartment, and was never away from the door until Katy agreed to go out with him, and now they are married.'

'A determined man; I like that,' Marcus offered, as he opened the passenger door of a sleek black car and ushered Eloise inside.

Starting the engine and driving off, Marcus shot her a brief sidelong glance and said, 'I intended taking you to a rather nice French restaurant, but I'm expecting a call from the west coast of America some time this evening so I've arranged for us to dine at my hotel. I hope you don't mind.'

Stilling a panicked shiver, Eloise cast a glance at his perfectly chiselled profile, Marcus wasn't a stranger and it wasn't their first date, so why was she hesitating?

'Eloise.' He flicked her a quizzical smile. 'It was either the hotel, or cancelling our dinner date.' It wasn't a lie— he was expecting a call—but also he wanted her on her own when he challenged her to explain her part in the scam her mother had pulled on his uncle.

'Yes, yes. That's perfectly all right.' She burst into speech. She was being stupid; she was twenty-four, not fourteen, and with a man who was no stranger to her, for heaven's sake, she told herself firmly.

The hotel was one of the best in London, and walking across the vast foyer with Marcus at her side, his hand gently at her elbow guiding her, she was glad she had taken time with her appearance. She was congratulating herself on her ability to mingle with the best, when Marcus stopped in front of a bank of elevators.

'Are we eating in the rooftop restaurant?' she asked, excitement bubbling in her veins. Walking into the elevator, she turned her sparkling green gaze up to his face adding, 'I've heard of it; the view is supposed to be marvellous.'

Intent dark eyes watched her apparently simple delight. 'Not exactly; we are dining in the penthouse suite,' Marcus drawled. 'But the view is equally as good. I know because I own the hotel.'

Involuntarily her jaw dropped. 'You own…your suite,' she stammered. The hotel dining room was one thing, but to be alone with Marcus in his suite was inviting intimacy… Eloise blushed scarlet at where her thoughts were leading, and her slim hands closed nervously together. But she could hardly object now, without looking like a fool.

Black-lashed ebony eyes skimmed over her tense figure, and finally settled on her burning cheeks. 'The call I am expecting is confidential,' Marcus murmured dryly. 'And your body language is very expressive,' he opined. 'I invited you to dinner, and you look like you expect to be the main course,' he chuckled.

Somehow his laughter eased her tension, and she walked into the elegant room, feeling much more confident. It was a vast room with a dining area. A table was already set with the finest linen and silverware. A few steps led down to the seating area where two large sofas flanked a low occasional table, and a massive glass wall looked out over the city.

'The bathroom is through there if you need it.' Marcus indicated with a wave of his hand to a large double door set in the rear wall. 'Have a seat while I order.'

She looked at the low sofas but opted to sit at the dining table.

In a matter of minutes Marcus had ordered the meal and a bottle of the best champagne and, after the wine waiter had filled their glasses and left, Marcus lifted his glass to Eloise. 'To the renewal of our friendship, and may I add you look enchanting.'

'Thank you.' Eloise blushed, her eyes meeting his across

the small table. His incredible eyes darkened for a second, and surprisingly she shivered.

'Cold?' Marcus asked.

'No, someone walked over my grave. I'm fine, really; it is the first day of spring.'

'Some spring in England!' Marcus teased. 'You must come to Greece for Easter. Now that *is* spring.' And he went into a description of the wild flowers on Rykos.

Over a meal of asparagus soup, followed by sea bass cooked in herbs and spices, the conversation flowed easily. Marcus was a witty and educated man, and Eloise gradually felt all her inhibitions disappear as she relaxed and fell deeper under his spell.

She refused a dessert but quite happily accepted yet another refill of champagne. When the dessert Marcus had ordered arrived, an incredible concoction of various ice creams, chocolate, nuts, and fruit, Eloise laughed out loud.

'You are never going to eat all that,' she prompted, grinning at the sheepish expression on his handsome face. 'It looks like a psychedelic leaning tower of Pisa.'

'Now you know my secret vice.' Marcus dipped the spoon into the glass, and lifted it out loaded with ice cream. 'I have a weakness for sweet things.' His dark eyes captured her amused green and, lifting the spoon to his mouth, he swallowed, then licked his lips with his tongue.

Suddenly the humour was gone, and heat curled in the pit of Eloise's stomach as she saw the muscle in the strong column of his throat move as he ate. There was something so very sensual about watching his obvious enjoyment, the tip of his tongue licking his firm lips.

'Want some?' Her green eyes widened and she saw the spoon he held out to her mouth. 'Go on, you will love it,' Marcus encouraged softly. 'It's good.'

There was nothing good about the gleam in the eyes

that held hers, but an explicit sexual promise. Involuntarily she moved slightly forward like a puppet on a string, and parted her lips. The ice cream tasted cool on her tongue, but her body heat shot up another notch.

Swallowing she jerked back and suddenly the air was filled with an electric tension. 'Very nice,' she mumbled.

'I told you so. Now have some more champagne.' He filled her glass yet again.

Eloise took another sip of the wine. Was she the only one who felt the simmering tension in the air? she wondered. And, desperate to get the conversation away from anything sexual, she asked. 'By the way, how is your Uncle Theo?'

Marcus stiffened. 'He died over twelve months ago in a car accident, leaving a wife and child.' He placed his glass back on the table.

Well, she had certainly succeeded in breaking the tension, Eloise thought ruefully, Marcus's face was like stone. 'Oh, I am sorry,' she mouthed her condolences.

'Why should you be? He was nothing to you; it was your sister, Chloe, who was his friend,' he said bluntly.

Scarlet colour burnt her cheeks, and whether it was the wine or nerves that made her do it she did not know. 'About Chloe...she wasn't my sister, she was my mother,' Eloise admitted, equally as blunt.

'Your mother? You do surprise me. Chloe didn't look old enough,' Marcus conceded, shooting her a veiled glance. It was a parody of innocence, he knew that. He had caught her by surprise last night and she had admitted her surname was different from her *sister's*. Obviously, rerunning yesterday's conversation in her mind, she had realised she had made a mistake, and her blushing revelation was damage limitation on her part. But, watching her, he wasn't so sure; her embarrassment looked genuine.

Relieved he had apparently taken her confession so well, a reflective smile curved Eloise's full lips. 'You're right. Chloe was only seventeen when she gave birth to me. That's why, when we hired the villa for a month, she insisted I pretend to be her sister.'

'But wasn't that hard for you? You were very young to have to lie all the time.' Marcus sympathised with an edge of irony in his tone and, reaching across the table, he took her hand in his in a comforting gesture.

'No, not really,' Eloise found herself admitting. 'I didn't know my mother very well. She divorced my father three months after marrying him, he disappeared and she married again quite quickly. My grandparents brought me up, while Chloe pursued a very successful career around the globe.'

His hand tightened on hers. 'So it was from your mother you got the desire to do well in business.'

'Yes, I suppose you could say that.' She hadn't thought of it that way, but he might be right. 'In fact, Chloe was very proud of my going to college, and if it hadn't been for her, Katy, Harry and I could never have made such a good start as we did.'

'How's that?'

'Well, with the money Chloe left me, we were able to set up business.'

So that was her story! Very plausible. Chloe's death lent weight to her words. God, but she was good, Marcus thought cynically. If he had not seen her name on the contract, he would have believed her himself.

'That must have helped to ease the pain of your mother's passing,' he said in a voice tinged with sarcasm.

'Yes and no.' She smiled a little sadly, and continued. 'But Harry said it was important, if you want to appeal to the top end of the market, to be in the right place, and he found the property in Mayfair and I made the downpayment on the Georgian house where we live and work.' She never realised what she was revealing as Marcus encouraged her to talk. She told him their dream of expanding the business throughout Europe, possibly the world.

'With your enthusiasm, I'm sure you will be very successful.' Marcus let go of her hand and, picking up the champagne bottle, refilled their glasses. Black lashes dropping down over his brilliant eyes, he added, 'A toast to your success and may you get everything you deserve.'

Eloise picked her glass up, and watched his strong brown fingers curl around the stem of his glass. He had wonderful hands, large but lean and powerful, and for a moment she had a vivid mental image of lying on a beach, and those same fingers tracing over her naked breasts. Her face suffused with heat as Marcus's voice broke into her erotic thoughts.

'And to a friendship rekindled.' Marcus touched his glass to hers, his gaze unwaveringly direct on her scarlet face.

'To success and friendship.' She smiled tentatively up at him, her green eyes wide and guileless. But it was a toast and a threat if she had but known it.

Marcus raised his glass and drained it. He could almost be fooled by her naïve innocence, her pleasure in the meal and the champagne. Damn it! She confused him like no other female. Once he made a decision he usually stuck by it, and yet he had changed his mind last night about Eloise and he was in danger of doing it again. Either the woman deserved an Oscar for her acting, or she really was unaware of her mother's trade. But then he recalled the elegant house she owned and, watching her sitting opposite him, she appeared to be modesty personified in a tailored suit that covered her and yet skilfully revealed between the edges of the jacket a glimpse of satin and an amber jewel lying enticingly in the shadow of a cleavage. She blushed like a teenager, while happily discussing expanding her business worldwide, and all these paradoxes made him want to shake her and demand that the real Eloise stand up.

A smile of wry self-mockery curved his firm mouth. Who was he kidding? First he would strip her naked and bury himself in her luscious body over and over again. The memory of her in his arms, the lush promise of her body that he had denied himself, had been a thorn in his side for far too long, and abruptly shoving back his chair he stood up.

Last night he had left a very angry, frustrated Nadine at her door, the picture of Eloise filling his mind. He had a damn good idea he was in for another night of frustration if he called Eloise a crook to her face, and the thought did not appeal.

CHAPTER THREE

ELOISE glanced up in surprise. What had she said wrong? He was towering over her, dark and vaguely dangerous, and she gave an inward sigh of relief when she saw a slow smile quirk the corners of his beautiful mouth. The evening had been magical so far and she wanted nothing to spoil it.

'There is only so long a man of my size can sit on a tiny gilt chair,' Marcus said ruefully, and casually he removed his jacket and loosened his shirt and tie, before adding, 'I need to stretch my legs and relax.'

Eloise swallowed hard. The white silk shirt fitted taut across his broad shoulders; the slightest tracing of dark body hair was visible beneath the fine fabric. His pants fitted snug on his hips and involuntarily her gaze strayed to his long legs. She could feel her temperature rising and it had nothing to do with the warmth of the room.

Luckily a knock on the door heralded the arrival of the waiter with the coffee and it gave Eloise a chance to get her breathing back to normal.

Marcus walked the few steps down to the lounging area, and indicated the low table to the waiter. 'Here, please, and you can take the rest away; we are finished.

'Come and join me, Eloise,' Marcus commanded softly.

Her hesitation was barely perceptible and, telling herself not to be so silly, she rose to her feet and walked down the few steps to join him.

'Let me take your jacket and make yourself comfortable.

I'll be mum—is that not an English saying?' he asked, one dark brow arching in enquiry.

She glanced up at him. 'Yes,' and she tried for a smile. She felt his hands curve around the front of her jacket and she gave a tiny compulsive shudder, suddenly intensely aware of the intimacy of their surroundings, the rising tension in the air around them.

'Allow me.' And slowly he parted the jacket across her body, the back of his hand brushing *accidentally* across her breasts.

Her reaction was instant, her breasts swelling beneath the fine fabric, and she gasped, shocked by her own response.

The jacket fell to the floor. Marcus felt her tremble and he saw the shadowing of arousal in her wide green eyes, and he did what he'd wanted to do from the moment he had seen her again.

He curved an arm around her tiny waist, his dark head dipped and he captured her mouth with his in a kiss of hungry possession. He felt her sudden tension, felt her lips clamp together in instinctive rejection, and deliberately he made his mouth gentle against hers. Using all his considerable sexual expertise, he slipped his other hand around the back of her head and, deftly unpinning her hair, he tangled it in the silken mass, keeping her head firm while his mouth brushed gently against hers, kissing and licking in a tantalising seduction.

Pressed into the hard heat of his body Eloise was vitally aware of every last lean muscular inch of him, and quivers of sexual tension shot through her body. She felt an insidious weakness stealing through her limbs. She should stop this, a tiny little voice in her head cried. But the fierce pounding of her heart and the sweet touch of his mouth on hers drowned the cry out.

Marcus sensed the instant she relaxed in his arms; she made a whimper of sound and he seized the moment to slip his tongue between her lips. She rose towards him, her arms closed around his neck, and slowly, almost tentatively, she returned his kiss.

The silken softness of her, the scent of her—something light and heady—rose to his nostrils and his body hardened. Reluctantly Marcus finally lifted his head, his breathing erratic, but the smile that curved his sensual mouth as his night-black eyes captured hers held an edge of triumph. He had discovered what he needed to know. Eloise still wanted him. She was his for the taking.

Eloise gazed helplessly up into his darkly attractive face, not knowing what had hit her. She ran the tip of her tongue over her swollen lips and swallowed convulsively. Marcus had kissed her, and she had responded—it was unbelievable, amazing!

'Do you want coffee or...?' he breathed against her cheek.

The invitation in the dark eyes that sought hers was explicit. Eloise blinked, her heart thundering in her chest. Dear heaven, she was tempted, very tempted, but something held her back. 'N-no, yes, n-no,' she stammered, and nervously jerked back from his restraining arm. The feelings, the reawakening of sexual urges long suppressed, were all too new and she needed time.

With a husky chuckle, Marcus pulled her back into his arms. 'If you can't decide, then let me help you.' He looked into her eyes. She wanted him, and he wanted her, wanted her with an ache, a hunger that blotted every sensible thought from his brain. So what if she was a liar and a cheat? At that moment he did not give a damn, and he brought his lips to hers again.

Slowly, warmth coursed through her veins again, until

her whole body was on fire for him. Somewhere in the darkest reaches of her brain she remembered she should be wary, but instead she marvelled at her own response as his mouth moved gently against hers in several nibbling little kisses that threatened to draw the breath from her body.

'You are so beautiful,' he murmured, burying his face in her hair. 'You're the most perfect woman I have ever seen.'

'No,' Eloise murmured but her voice was shaky, and when Marcus brushed the hair away from her neck, and began kissing his way down her neck, lingering on the pulse that beat madly beneath her pale skin, she moaned.

'Yes,' Marcus whispered, and kissed her again.

Involuntarily her lips parted to accept the persuasive invasion of his tongue. She trembled, both hands clutching desperately at his broad shoulders, her feminine form reaching out, reacting to the lure of his potent sensuality.

Her breasts were swollen, her nipples tight aching buds, and she writhed against the hard male body, painfully aware of the restriction of the two fine layers of fabric preventing the flesh-on-flesh contact she craved.

His tongue delved deeper in her mouth, and he kissed with a fierce sexual passion that made every cell in her body pulsate in one tumultuous flood of feeling. If he had not been holding her, she would have collapsed.

A sharp whimper of need escaped her as he lifted his dark head; his eyes, black as jet, stared down into hers, and then he deliberately moved against her, letting her feel the hard evidence of his arousal. 'The bedroom, Eloise.' One hand slipped round to cup her breast. 'Say yes,' he husked, as his thumb stoked the rigid tip through the soft silk covering.

She heard the words and she knew what he was asking;

and in a flash of blinding clarity she knew this was her one chance for love. Her one chance to know a man—and not just any man, but Marcus. The only man she had ever loved.

She leant into the hard heat of him, and twined her arms around his neck. 'Yes,' she breathed unsteadily, as he swept her off her feet and carried her into the bedroom.

The room was in semi-darkness; only a bedside lamp shed a small pool of light over a large king-sized bed. The bed penetrated her haze of passion and fear flickered in her eyes but, before she could mouth the words of protest that trembled on her tongue, Marcus laid her down on the bed, stripping her skirt and top from her heated body in between kisses with a deftness that left her breathless.

She started to get up and stopped as, with stunning speed, Marcus shed his clothes. Half fascinated, half fearful, she could not tear her gaze away from his naked form. Shaking, she rested on her elbows. He was so perfect, so magnificently male, a tanned, hard, muscular chest with a light dusting of black hair that tapered down over a flat stomach, and lower... She gulped and swallowed hard, her green eyes flying back to his face as he joined her on the bed.

He loomed over her, his handsome face above hers taut, his dark eyes black and gleaming with a passion, a fire that reminded her of the past.

She was nineteen again and reached up for him, and then his mouth was hot, demanding everything with such hungry intensity she knew she should be frightened. But she did not have time to be afraid as caressing fingers curved around her breasts, and then hot hard kisses trailed down her throat, and a hungry male mouth fastened over the peak of one perfectly formed breast. Her back arched and she groaned out loud as he rendered the same treatment to her other breast.

'You like that,' Marcus rasped.

Eloise whispered his name as she wound her arms tightly around his neck. Her hands stroked his silken hair, and down over his powerful shoulders. Then he captured her mouth again in a long drugging kiss. When he broke the kiss and reared back, her slender arms fell from his shoulders and she felt bereft. Instinctively, she reached out to rest her hands on his chest. Her need to touch him was uncontrollable.

Breathing heavily, Marcus quickly removed the last barrier of delicate lacy briefs and stared down at her. She was so exquisite, so beautiful, her high round breasts with perfect deep rose peaks that begged for a man's mouth, the smooth curve of her waist, the feminine flare of her hips, and the red curling crest that he had ached for so long to discover. He wanted her, he wanted to touch, to taste every inch of her, to bury himself deep in the hot moist centre of her, until she cried out his name in ecstasy and she was truly his.

He closed his hands over hers and lifted them above her head, as he slowly lowered his head and kissed her mouth until it opened to his. He rubbed his chest against her breasts, glorying in the friction, and triumphant at her shuddering response. He cupped her breasts in his hands and rolled each taut nipple between his fingers. His black eyes sought hers, and he murmured, 'Perfect.'

Eloise had never imagined such pleasure existed, and she moved blindly against him. His hand slipped down to her belly and lower to her thighs, and she tensed.

Marcus sensed some resistance beneath Eloise's headlong response, and he vowed he would wait even if it killed him. He had once promised her it would be perfect and he intended to fulfil the promise. He bent his head towards her and tongued each rigid-tipped breast, and then drew her flesh in his mouth.

Eloise gasped his name, 'Marcus,' as his fingers gently stroked between her thighs, slowly, lightly. She felt electric shock-waves of sensation jolting through her body; she wanted him, and she wanted to cry out, but instead she pressed her mouth to his throat and bit down in a fever of frustration.

Marcus stifled a groan and the swift kiss he pressed on her love-swollen lips turned into a savage duelling of tongues, as his long fingers parted the petals of her woman-hood and found the hot, damp, velvet flesh throbbing, waiting for him...

He touched her gently, softly, fast then slow, until her hips arched towards him, and her hands dug into his shoulders and she was calling out his name.

Eloise shook violently, a fierce tension she had never experienced before jerking her every nerve and muscle tight, driving every single thought from her head, and leaving only a fiery need that was almost pain. 'Please,' she moaned, her head thrashing from side to side. His hands slipped under her hips and lifted her clear of the bed. She felt the velvet tip of his hard male flesh stroke and then with one thrust he was there, where she wanted him to be.

Eloise felt the briefest of pains, and then it happened. Marcus's great body stilled for a second in disbelief.

She moaned his name and he moved deep and hard, filling her, stretching her, and taking her on a wild journey of almost mystical proportion. She felt the mighty strength of him thrusting, driving her on, until she cried out as her slender body convulsed in a paroxysm of sensation, and he joined with her until she had lost all sense of self, and the two of them became one perfect whole.

Afterwards she lay in his arms and felt the light caress of his fingertips against her sweat-damped flesh, soothing and caressing; he was murmuring husky words in Greek she did not understand. She sighed her delight, then tensed as his fingers found the ridge of flesh forming a scar on her inner thigh.

'What is this?' Marcus asked lazily, leaning over her and, by the dim light, let his slumberous eyes sweep over her beautiful naked body to where his fingers had found a small ridge of flesh. One long shapely leg had a scar about four inches long almost at the top.

'Nothing.' Eloise tried to cross her legs suddenly embarrassed. 'Just a scar. I'm sorry if it upsets you.'

'Oh, no, sweetheart,' Marcus exclaimed and smiled down at her. 'It does not upset me; in fact it is rather endearing. A tiny blemish in such perfection makes you seem more human,' he opined, and brushed her lips with his. 'But how did it happen? You did not have it when you were nineteen.'

'No... well...' She hesitated, and swallowed hard. 'I was locked out of my apartment and I broke a window to get in, and cut my leg—nothing serious.'

'Nothing serious,' he murmured, moving down her naked body; he let his fingers trace the scar, feeling anger for her accident, and fiercely protective. As his woman there would be no more accidents, he vowed, and his lips followed the path of his fingers. This time the loving was slow and tender, but the end was the same, one perfect unity.

Eloise curled up close and wrapped her arms around his neck. She did not want to think about the past. She did not want to think about anything except how much she loved this man. Tonight had been a revelation and, for the first time in her life, she knew what it was to be a woman, and it was all because of Marcus. She hugged him, finally admitting to herself she had never got over him. She had loved him as a teenager, and she loved him now and probably always would, and a contented sigh escaped her.

'Sighing. I didn't think I was that bad,' Marcus prompted and tilted her chin with a finger, his dark eyes gleaming down into hers.

'That was a happy sigh,' she speedily corrected him and, lifting a finger, she placed it over his lips. 'And you know it, Buster. I can see smug male triumph in your eyes,' she teased back.

'Cheeky.' He grinned broadly. 'But I...' Whatever he was going to say was cut off by the loud ringing of the telephone.

Hauling himself off the bed, Marcus picked up the phone from the bedside table, and as Eloise watched the laughing teasing lover vanished and the hard-headed businessman took his place. He was talking in Greek, and when he finally put the phone down he turned to Eloise. 'Sorry about that.'

'You really were expecting a call.' She had had her doubts, and it was nice to know he had not tricked her into his suite, and bed.

'O, ye of little faith,' he mocked with a grin. 'Actually, I have to make another one and, much as I would love to spend the night with you, I'd better get you back before your friends wonder what has happened to you.'

She wrinkled her nose at him. 'I am a grown woman.'

He planted a kiss on the tip of her nose, 'And if I stay here much longer I will be a grown man,' he drawled sexily. Eloise blushed at his innuendo, and Marcus laughed out loud. 'For a sophisticated lady, you blush delightfully.'

'It's the bane of my life,' she admitted with a grin. 'The penalty for being a redhead, I suppose.'

Marcus sent her a flashing smile of pure male satisfaction. 'A natural one, as I now know, but if I don't make this call my penalty is going to be the loss of a rather large deal.'

'Heaven forbid, business first.'

He gave her a playful shove. 'And you can have the bathroom first, and if you're lucky I might join you.'

Eloise shot him a startled glance and, swinging her legs over the side of the bed, she grasped the sheet and pulled it around her. She caught Marcus's husky chuckle, but she wasn't brave enough to parade in front of him naked—yet. She walked across to the bathroom door and turned. Her green eyes sparkling, she drawled, 'Promises, promises,' with a shake of her beautiful head. She could joke because she felt so great. He hadn't said he loved her, but she was sure he did, and they had all the time in the world to get to know each other.

But in that she was wrong.

Five minutes later she walked back into the bedroom, and there was no sign of Marcus. Quickly she slipped back into her rather crumpled clothes, and wandered through into the sitting room.

Almost dressed, he was shrugging his broad shoulders into the jacket of his suit. He looked heartbreakingly handsome, and Eloise wanted to fling herself into his arms. Instead she picked up her own jacket and slipped it on, suddenly shy.

'Sorry, Eloise.' He strode towards her. 'But the call was a bit more complicated than I had envisaged.' He slid a comforting arm around her shoulder. 'I'd better get you home.' His dark eyes rueful, he looked down at her. 'I need to get on to the computer.'

'Oh.'

Marcus noted the crestfallen expression on her lovely

face. 'I'll call you tomorrow. I promise.' And as he said
it he knew it was true. He wanted this woman far more
than any other woman he had ever met, and he did not
want the relationship compromised by what to him was a
paltry sum of money.

He was Greek, and honour and pride meant a lot. He
had been very close to his Uncle Theo, who had been taken
for a fool by Chloe Baker, and, sure Eloise had benefited
from her mother's scam—in fact all the evidence suggested she was in on the scam with Chloe. But it did not
follow that she would do the same on her own. He had
made some calls today and, as far as he could ascertain,
Eloise worked hard at a successful business and, unlike
her mother, she was not known for granting sexual favours
to men, while conning them out of money.

Why spoil what promised to be a great affair by seeking
monetary revenge? Everyone was entitled to one mistake
in life, and she had been very young. His mind made up,
he gathered Eloise into his arms, and kissed her. 'Forgive
me,' he murmured against her cheek.

Staring up at him, Eloise was astonished to see a flicker
of vulnerability in his lustrous black eyes, and her heart
swelled with love. He was actually worried about leaving
her, proof that he really cared. 'Of course, Marcus, always.' She lifted a finger to his lips. 'Don't worry. You
forget I have a business to run myself—I understand.'

If only he could... 'Yes, I know,' Marcus said shortly,
his arm dropping from her shoulder to curve round her
elbow and lead her to the door.

Sensing the tension in his huge frame, she tried hard to
reassure him as they went down in the elevator. 'Actually,
I am going to be very busy myself. We are expanding and
opening a branch in Paris.'

'Isn't that rather sudden?' Marcus queried, urging her out of the elevator and into the hotel foyer.

Eloise's glance flew up to meet dark enigmatic eyes. 'Not really. After dinner last night, Ted and I stayed on to watch the show, and had a real fun evening. We danced and joked and Ted agreed to invest the money to expand KHE in principle.' She grinned up at Marcus. 'It was great, but it was three before I got home, and then we talked over the possibilities of opening in Paris. Ted actually knows of some great premises that are available.'

By *we* Eloise meant Katy and Harry, but Marcus drew a totally different conclusion. His dark eyes blazed with savage violence that Eloise was totally unaware of; she had no idea of the effect her rambling explanation was having on the man at her side.

'It was so exciting, it was after five before I finally got to sleep, then this morning we signed the deal, and went out for lunch to celebrate.' The enthusiasm in her tone was unmistakable. This had been one of the best days of her life—success in business, and in love.

A muscle knotted in Marcus's jaw. *Home at three and finally asleep at five!* It did not take Einstein to work out what she had been doing, and yet he could have sworn he was her first lover, more fool him... He'd been wrong about Eloise—and he'd been taken in by her beguiling act. Just like Ted had.

'You've planned everything out pretty carefully, I see. Good for you,' he grated, lashing himself into a fury at her deceit, made all the more powerful by the fact that an hour ago he'd been willing to forgive the damn woman anything.

Yet by her own admission she'd spent the night with Ted Charlton, persuaded him into parting with the money she wanted and rounded the date off with lunch. Eloise was exactly like her mother. Her sexy body had addled his brain, but no more… This time she was going to pay…

'Get in the car,' he said between gritted, even white teeth.

Eloise never noticed the icy anger in his eyes as he leant over her and fastened her seat belt. She simply wallowed in the heavenly scent of his magnificent male body, and finally realised what animal magnetism was really all about.

The car stopped before the entrance of her home, and she turned to Marcus but he was already out and walking around the front of the car. He opened the passenger door and held out his hand. Trustingly Eloise curled her fingers around the firm warmth of his palm, as she straightened and they walked to the door.

'You have your key?'

'Yes.' Reluctantly, she let go of his hand while she extracted the key from her purse and inserted it in the lock. She glanced up at him uncertainly. 'Do you want to come in?'

'No, I have to dash.'

He was a tall, broad silhouette outlined by the streetlight, his features in shadow, and for a moment she wondered what lay behind the dark mask of his face. And what was the protocol when you had slept with a man? Suddenly she was nervous for no reason. 'Well, thank you for a lovely evening,' she said softly, and stupidly offered her hand.

'I think we are past the handshaking stage, Eloise, way past,' Marcus drawled mockingly, making no attempt to take her hand. 'I'll be in touch. But I think I might have to go to America for a while.'

Her heart sank. She might not see him again for weeks.

'Promise,' she demanded urgently; there was something about the cool remote look in his eyes that worried her.

One dark brow arched sardonically. 'Oh, I promise, Eloise.' With a speed that left her breathless, he hauled her into his arms, and kissed her with a savagery that left her reeling. He spun on his heel and was opening the car door before she could say good night.

CHAPTER FOUR

'So what do you think?' Eloise did a pirouette, showing off the black strapless cocktail dress with a skirt that ended a good three inches above her knees, clinging to every curve of her body in between. 'The new me.' Her green eyes laughing, she sought the opinion of Katy, who was sitting on Eloise's sofa a bit like a beached whale, her eyes wide as saucers.

It was Saturday evening and Eloise had spent the whole day shopping for a complete new wardrobe, and for the past hour she had modelled them all for Katy.

'I'm stunned. They are all gorgeous—quite a metamorphosis from the perennial student to an elegant woman, and not before time.'

'I know.' Eloise sat down beside Katy on the sofa. 'I never really felt the need, what with working and living here, plus I don't feel so guilty spending money on myself, now I know Ted Charlton is backing us thanks to you and Harry.'

'Don't thank us,' Katy said, staggering to her feet. 'In my opinion, your new dress sense has little to do with the business expanding, and more to do with a dark-eyed Greek, and I'm glad for you. But be careful.'

Eloise felt the colour rise in her cheeks. Katy was right, but since her dinner date with Marcus her whole attitude had changed. It was four days since she had dined with him, made love with him, and she was missing him quite dreadfully. She only had to think of the kisses they'd shared to be able to taste him on her lips, and when she thought of the rest, her body burned. She could hardly believe the transformation from celibate female to the hungry, needy woman she had become, but she liked it. She felt like a teenager again, and jumped every time the telephone rang.

'Did you hear what I said?' Katy chuckled at the dreamy expression on her partner's face. 'Be careful.'

'I don't know what you're talking about; I only had dinner once with the man.' She had not told Katy everything! 'As for being careful—' Eloise got to her feet '—aren't I always?' she murmured dryly. 'Come on, I'll help you back down stairs. Harry should be back soon.'

The door slamming and a voice yelling 'Katy' made the two women smile.

'Speak of the devil.' Eloise laughed as she helped Katy down to her apartment.

Half an hour later, Eloise walked back up to her own place. Harry had returned from Paris, having completed the deal on the property to expand the business. Everything was going great, and all it needed to make Eloise's life perfect was for Marcus to return.

Relaxing by the telephone on Sunday evening, if one could call it relaxing, as she lived in hope Marcus would call, Eloise idly leafed through the morning paper. Her hand stilled, and her happy state of anticipation, took a nosedive. Her stomach turned in a nauseous roll, her eyes fixed on the glossy photograph in the celebrity section. Marcus Kouvaris with his beautiful companion Nadine snapped at a charity ball in London on Thursday evening. The night after he had taken Eloise out...

Eloise stared at the image of a devastatingly attractive Marcus in a black dinner suit, smiling at the tall blonde hanging on to his arm, and wanted to weep. What a fool she was. Floating on cloud nine, imagining a relationship with Marcus Kouvaris, dreaming impossible dreams of love, and even marriage, rushing out and buying a whole new wardrobe on the strength of *'I'll call you'*... She ground her teeth together in angry frustration at her own lunatic behaviour.

Slowly, like an old woman, she got to her feet, the paper dropping unnoticed to the floor, and made her way to the bedroom. Her eyes filled with moisture. She flopped down on the bed and let the tears fall. She had vowed at nineteen never to cry over another man again. Strictly speaking, she had not broken her vow, she thought between sobs as she was crying over the same man. But didn't that make her an even bigger idiot?

She rolled over onto her stomach, buried her face in the pillow and sobbed her heart out. Her slender body shook with the force of her grief.

Finally, all cried out, she turned over onto her back, and with sightless eyes gazed at the ceiling. She could remember every touch, every kiss, the awe, the wonder she'd felt when he'd finally possessed her. But what for her had been a miracle, for Marcus had obviously been simply another roll in the hay. When she finally slept a tall dark man haunted her dreams, and she cried out in her sleep.

Work was Eloise's salvation, but even that did not occupy her every waking hour, and she found herself making excuses for the man. Perhaps his date with Nadine was innocent, perhaps he would still ring her—and she despised herself for her weakness.

But as March gave way to April, and then May, and Marcus never contacted her again, finally Eloise accepted it was history repeating itself. Marcus had forgotten all about her. She and Katy worked flat out to build up a whole new range for the Paris branch and work stopped her brooding over Marcus.

Katy gave birth to a fine baby boy, Benjamin, and Eloise found herself more involved in the business side than ever. But designing was her strong point so they decided to employ two more staff—a young man, Peter, fresh out of college, to help with the actual making of the pieces, and then there was Floe Brown, a woman in her fifties who wanted to get back into work after being out of the job market for years, who was an absolute gem. When not helping Harry in the office she quite happily looked after the baby and let Katy work; it was a brilliant arrangement.

Eloise had reason to be grateful for her new clothes, even if she had bought them with one particular man in mind. Surprisingly she discovered they gave her a growing confidence in herself. Because of Katy's involvement with her new baby, Eloise, who had left the publicity aspect of the business to Katy and Harry, now found she was more involved with the setting up of the Paris boutique, doing interviews, and socialising with the ultra-chic French. A welcome spin-off was she actually developed a veneer of sophistication that effectively masked her naturally very private nature.

It was a warm June afternoon, and just two hours to the grand opening of KHE of Paris. Eloise glanced around the elegant shop with a professional eye. The jewellery on display was some of their best work and, fingers crossed, she prayed the new outlet would be a success. They had spent an awful lot of money and taken on quite a debt, but according to Harry it was manageable. It had better be, she thought dryly, or they might all end up out on the street, instead of in the plush hotel where they had spent the last two days getting everything ready.

'Right, Jeff. I'm leaving you in charge; don't touch anything, and don't start on the champagne. Katy, Harry and I will be back by five-thirty, ready to open the doors for the preview at six. Okay?'

'Stop fussing; go and make yourself beautiful. Julian is determined to get some really stunning photographs tonight for the glossy mags. If even half the people invited turn up it will be a great success, so stop worrying.'

Standing in front of the bathroom mirror in her hotel an hour later, Eloise could not help worrying. Outlining her full lips with one last coat of lip-gloss, she patted them with a tissue, and stepped back. Her red hair was piled high on the top of her head in a coronet of curls. Her make-up was subtle, a touch of eye-shadow and eyeliner accentuated her wide green eyes, her thick lashes held the lightest trace of mascara, and a light moisturiser was all she needed. Around her throat she wore a glittering jade and jet choker that draped down her breastbone in a waterfall of intricately cut beads, one of her own designs, and displayed perfectly against her pale skin. Matching earrings and a wide bracelet around her slender wrist completed the set.

Eloise ran her hands down her hips, smoothing the fabric of the simple black strapless sheath dress she was wearing over her thighs, to where it ended some way above her knees.

Yes, Katy had been right, it was the perfect foil for the jewellery, Eloise thought musingly and, leaving the bathroom, she picked up her purse and headed for Katy's hotel room.

'At last,' Harry blurted as he opened the door at Eloise's knock. 'We're going to be late for our own opening.'

'Don't panic.' Eloise looked at his frazzled expression, and wanted to laugh. 'I'm sure everything will be fine.'

And it was, Eloise thought some three hours later looking around the crowded room. The two French staff they had employed were being kept busy. Julian was happily taking shots of at least four supermodels, and a handful of the top French designers were present, plus a lot of their very wealthy clients.

The jewellery had been admired and sold, plus they had taken a highly satisfactory number of orders and one elderly lady had even tried to buy the set Eloise was wearing. The champagne and canapés seemed to be holding out, and she allowed herself a small sigh of pleasure as she took a sip of champagne. The first drink she'd had, as she'd wanted to keep a clear head.

'I told you, Eloise—' Ted Charlton appeared at her side '—you have a winner, no doubt about it.'

'I hope so, for your sake as well as ours.' She smiled at the burly American.

'Oh, I'm not bothered,' Ted said, and in abrupt change of subject added, 'how well do you know Marcus Kouvaris?'

She stiffened. 'I had dinner with him a while ago. I suppose you could say we are friends.' The fact she had hoped they could be a lot more still had the power to hurt her, and with a dismissive shrug of her slender shoulders she made herself add lightly. 'Or perhaps acquaintances would be a better word.'

'Good, good, that's what I thought.' The obvious relief in his tone was plain.

'Why do you ask?' she demanded.

Ted took a glass of champagne from a passing waiter, and gulped it down, before turning his attention back to Eloise. 'I'm taking you out to dinner later. We'll talk then, okay?'

She liked the older man and she didn't want to make

an issue out of a casual question, especially not about Marcus. 'Okay, Ted.' She grinned.

'Great,' and, patting her shoulder, he moved off into the crowd.

Eloise shook her head, Ted was half drunk already and, draining her own glass, she turned and placed it on the table behind her.

'Hello, Ted, great to see you again.'

Eloise recognised the deep, slightly accented voice above the hum of the crowd, and shock froze her to the spot. It was Marcus Kouvaris. What was he doing here? She certainly hadn't invited him. Though she might have done if he'd ever bothered to keep in touch, her own innate honesty forced her to admit, as she fought to control her pounding heart.

How long she stood with her back to the crowd, she had no idea, but finally schooling her features into a polite social mask she turned around, head high, and let her glance roam apparently idly over the room. Then she saw him. His dark head was bent towards one of the models, apparently listening to what the woman was saying.

He was easily the tallest man present and, with his dark good looks, and wearing an immaculately tailored light-weight beige suit, he stood out from the crowd. Eloise could not take her eyes off him; animal magnetism didn't cover it, she thought helplessly. Whatever *it* was, Marcus had it in spades.

Suddenly he lifted his head and night-black eyes clashed with hers and just as suddenly Eloise had the totally un-ladylike desire to yell at him? 'Where the hell have you been for the past three months?' Of course she didn't, but instead she managed a stiff smile, before tearing her gaze from his.

She feigned interest in the elderly lady who was once

again admiring her necklace, but without hearing a word the poor dear was saying.

A large hand lightly brushed her forearm, to attract her attention; her head jerked up. It was Marcus at her side. Keep it cool, you're a sophisticated businesswoman, she told herself firmly. So what if she had a one-night stand with the man? She wasn't the first and she certainly would not be the last where a sexual predator like Marcus Kouvaris was concerned. She had no illusions on that score, and though he didn't know it he'd done her a favour...

'Marcus, what a surprise. I thought you would be far too busy to attend this sort of thing,' she opined lightly.

'Ah, Eloise, would I miss your opening?' he prompted his dark eyes holding a glint of wicked humour. 'I'm only sorry I didn't get in touch sooner.' His smile was disarming. 'But pressure of work.' He gave a shrug of his broad shoulders. 'That's how it goes sometimes.'

'Yes, of course.' Eloise couldn't say anything else under the circumstances. She had no claim on the man. So he had taken her to bed and taken her virginity? What did that matter to a devil like Marcus?

'I knew you would understand.' His eyes captured hers, faintly mocking beneath hooded lids, and the breath caught in her throat.

'Yes, well, I'm an understanding kind of girl,' she managed in a weak attempt at humour.

'You are also a very beautiful one.' Marcus moved slightly, the sleeve of his jacket brushing her arm. 'You look fantastic.' With casual ease, he reached out and lifted the waterfall of beads at her throat, and let them trail through his long fingers. 'Your design?'

He was much too close. The heady masculine scent of him, the touch of his fingers on her flesh, sent heat flooding through every vein in her body. She swallowed hard, and stepped back. 'Yes.'

'Exquisite.' His hand fell from her throat. 'Congratulations, Eloise. It looks like your latest venture will be a great success.'

With a bit of space between them, Eloise felt slightly more in control. 'Thank you. We hope so,' she responded with a baring of her teeth that she hoped would pass for a smile, and glimpsed a flash of mockery in the dark eyes that held her own.

'Can there be a doubt? After all, Eloise, your mother was highly successful, and you obviously have her talent.' A talent for squeezing money out of men, Marcus thought grimly. But she had other talents, he recognised, as he looked down at her. She was one gorgeous, sexy lady, as he knew only too well, but she was also a liar and a devious little thief. Yet even now if he saw just one genuine smile from her luscious lips, he would probably forgive her everything, and he despised himself for it.

'You think so?'

'Oh, I know so,' he said with the arch of one perfect ebony brow. 'But let's cut out the niceties and get down to what really interests me.' The gleam in his eyes, as he surveyed her slender figure from the top of her head to her toes, left her in no doubt as to what he meant.

Eloise fought down the blush that threatened and said, 'Actually, I'm surprised to see you here. I don't remember inviting you.'

'You didn't. Ted Charlton did.'

Eloise stared up at him, her green eyes puzzled. 'I didn't realise you knew him that well.'

A smile touched his hard mouth. 'You'd be surprised. But let's not talk about Ted; let's talk about you. I suppose it's too much to hope you are still unattached. There must be lots of men in Paris all vying for your attention.'

'I don't think that's any business of yours.' She hid a wry smile, thinking of the twenty-hour days she had worked to get the Paris shop started.

'I thought we were friends.' His gaze was unwaveringly direct 'More than friends.' His deep voice dropped seductively. 'After this is over, let me take you out to dinner and show you.'

For sheer arrogant conceit, he took the biscuit, Eloise thought furiously. He had slept with her, dropped her like a hot potato, and casually walked back into her life, uninvited, months later, and thought he could seduce her all over again. What kind of fool did he take he for? He might be incredibly handsome, and incredibly rich, but he was also a womanising bastard, as she knew to her cost.

'Thank you for the invite, but no, thanks. I already have a dinner date.'

One black brow lifted sardonically. 'Shame. Perhaps some other time, as I remember the last time we dined together you seemed to enjoy my company, and I know I enjoyed you.'

Hot colour stained her cheeks. How dared he remind her of that? She wanted to knock the cynical smile off his rotten face. Her hands curled into tight fists at her sides, and she was rigid with anger... But, remembering where she was, with the greatest difficulty she controlled herself.

'Eloise, isn't it marvellous?' Katy was Eloise's salvation.

Turning her back on Marcus, her gaze flew to her friend's face. Katy looked amused and excited, whereas she felt embarrassed. 'Yes, great.'

'For heaven's sake, lighten up, Eloise. We're a success. Enjoy it, and introduce me to this marvellous man.'

Eloise almost groaned out loud. Marcus had positioned himself at her side, and was standing there, oozing charm... The snake! But she had no choice but to make the introductions. She watched cynically as Marcus, with a few well-chosen words that flattered Katy's beauty and business sense, charmed her friend completely.

'You've met Harry, I believe,' Eloise said as Harry joined the group.

'Yes, the first time guarding the door in London, and I can't say I blame you, Harry, with two such stunningly attractive woman to look after.'

'Your chauvinism is showing,' Katy quipped, and they all laughed.

'Then let me apologise by taking you all to dinner.'

'No, no.' Ted appeared. 'Tonight is my treat. Eloise has already agreed but, hey, why don't you all come—and you too, Marcus? It will save time.'

'Eloise?' Katy deferred, and the decision was hers.

Save time for what? Eloise briefly wondered but, pinning a smile on her face, she said, 'Yes, the more, the merrier.' But inside she was fuming. And what did Marcus mean by *'the first time he had met Harry'*? To her knowledge he had only met Harry once. Was Marcus having a sly dig at her? Her paranoia was showing. Marcus Kouvaris was not worth thinking about.

'Come on, then,' Harry cried. 'Let's thank and say goodbye to our guests. Jeff and Julian can close up. We have already overrun half an hour, and I am not used to eating late; my stomach feels as if my throat is cut.'

General laughter followed, and an hour later saw the five of them seated at a table next to the small dance floor in a nightclub in the Latin Quarter, enjoying a jovial meal.

'I'm stuffed,' Katy groaned, eyeing the last remnants of a huge cream concoction. 'And if I don't get back to the hotel soon, our son will be screaming for his feed, and Floe will be pulling her hair out.'

'Before you decide to leave,' Ted cut in, 'I have something to tell you.'

The meal had been torture for Eloise, who'd been trying to behave cool and unconcerned by Marcus's presence. Forced to watch him win over Katy with his wit and easy charm, when she wanted to yell he was a rat... She gave an inward sigh of relief when Katy proposed leaving—her ordeal was almost over. But she was wrong. It was just beginning...

'Katy, Eloise, I have an announcement to make,' Ted declared.

Glancing at Ted, Eloise, saw the almost conspiratorial look he exchanged with Harry and Marcus, and Marcus's head dipped slightly in a nod of assent. She looked from one to the other, an uneasy suspicion she was not going to like Ted's revelation making her stiffen in her seat.

'I have sold my share in KHE to Marcus here.' Ted gestured expansively with the wave of his brandy glass. 'He made me an offer I couldn't refuse and, before you girls start worrying, let me assure you Marcus is committed to investing double the amount I gave you. Expansion into New York, if you like.' He beamed around the table. 'A great deal all round, isn't it, Harry?'

The announcement hit Eloise like a punch in the stomach. It turned her to stone. She could feel the blood slowly draining from her face, and the panicked increase in her heartbeat. Marcus as a partner—not the kind she had once dreamed, a marriage partner, but a business partner. She glanced at him, and he returned her look without a flicker of emotion showing on his hard features. She searched his hooded dark eyes, but found nothing other than an arched eyebrow at her scrutiny. Why? Why on earth would Marcus buy into their business?

'You knew about this?' Eloise heard Katy demand of Harry, and glanced across the table at her two friends.

'Yes, but I didn't want to worry you with business when you had our baby to look after and all the extra work Eloise had to do. Plus the deal was only finalised three days ago, and we wanted no hint of changing partners so near to the Paris opening. You know what the press are like—the least hint of instability and the rumours would fly.'

Marcus took charge in his indomitable manner. 'Your husband is right, Katy. I have no intention of interfering in any way with your work. You and Eloise will have complete artistic freedom.' Turning his attention from Katy to Eloise, his black lashed glittering eyes trailed over her tense figure, lingering on the curve of her breasts and finally slowly back up to her pale face to trap her angry green eyes. 'I promise,' he vowed softly, 'I will simply be a sleeping partner, a sleeping partner who provides the money, when and where it is needed.' He smiled, a brief curl of his lips.

Eloise's slender hands closed convulsively together on her lap. He sat there, cool, calm, and immensely self-assured, and only she could see the smile never reached his eyes, but contempt and a glint of sexual menace glimmered in the black depths.

'It will be fine, Eloise,' Harry piped up.

'You should have discussed it. I mean, Ted is, was…' Eloise floundered wildly for a moment with a glance at the now thoroughly drunk Ted. He was no help, she realised with a sinking feeling in the pit of her stomach. One look at Katy talking animatedly on the side to Marcus, and she knew Katy had already accepted the deal. Her friend would never go against her husband in any case.

'Are you all right with this new arrangement, Eloise?' Katy finally asked, her brown eyes sparkling. 'Personally, I think it's an incredible opportunity.'

An opportunity for whom? Eloise wondered. And did they have a choice?

'Yes. You're probably right,' she conceded. A steel band of tension was now throbbing across her head, and she took very little part in the ensuing conversation, her thoughts and emotions in chaos.

It didn't make sense. If Marcus had cared for her, she could perhaps understand him investing in KHE. But he hadn't contacted her in over three months. So why? The question went around and around in her brain.

Another bottle of champagne and another round of toasts were drunk to the new partnership, and everyone congratulated everyone else. While Eloise had to battle to keep a smile on her face, her lips were numb with the effort.

'I know I said I would not interfere in the running of the business.' Marcus's comment made Eloise sit up and take notice.

'But KHE is a bit of an obscure title for designer jewellery. No disrespect to you, Katy and Harry, but did you never consider something like, "Eloise by Design"? It has a much more sophisticated ring to it.' Marcus dropped the original name invented by Chloe and Eloise into the conversation, and watched with narrowed eyes as all the colour faded from Eloise's face. She looked as guilty as sin, exactly as he'd expected. Though he hadn't expected the overlong tense pause, and he turned his attention to Katy. She was staring at Eloise with a mixture of horror and *sympathy*! There was something between them Marcus did not understand...

'We did consider it,' Katy answered. 'But decided we preferred the more enigmatic KHE. We thought it sounds like "key," and the key to a well-dressed woman is the jewellery she wears.'

Eloise gave an inward sigh of relief when Marcus appeared to accept the explanation and asked Katy to dance. At least it would get him away from the table, and give her a chance to try and get her thoughts into some kind of order and make sense of the evening's proceedings.

'No, sorry, Marcus. Harry and I are responsible parents now. It's time we called a taxi and got back to our son. And, by the look of Ted, we'd better take him with us. He doesn't look capable of making his own way back to the hotel.'

'What about you, Eloise?' Marcus queried, turning his head to glance down at her by his side. 'The night is still young. Shall we dance?' His dark eyes lit with amusement and something else she did not want to acknowledge dared her to agree. 'Or are you going to desert me as well?'

Eloise felt the colour surge in her cheeks, and prayed no one noticed. She had been supremely conscious of Marcus all through the meal. The occasional brush of his thigh against hers beneath the table, the apparently friendly gesture when he placed his hand on her arm when making a point, the rub of his shoulder against her when he leant forward to fill Katy's wine glass. He hadn't singled her out particularly, but he'd managed to arouse her to a state of tension without even trying. It was only the presence of her friends that had allowed her to retain a modicum of self-control. Until Ted had dropped his bombshell—and she was still trying to get her head around the fact that Marcus had bought into the company. Dancing with the man was the last thing she wanted. 'No…' She began to make her excuse.

'Of course she will,' Katy cut in, rising to her feet along with Harry and Ted. 'Eloise has been working like a slave for months; she deserves some fun.' Katy answered before Eloise could mouth her refusal. 'She is staying here for a couple of days to sort out any teething troubles, so a late night won't kill her.'

'Do you mind?' Eloise finally found her voice. 'I can speak for myself,' she shot back.

'I know, Eloise,' Katy responded, suddenly serious. 'I'm sorry.'

Marcus glanced back from one woman to the other and for the second time that evening thought there was something going on between them, but dismissed the notion when Eloise spoke.

'Don't apologise.' Lifting defiant green eyes to Marcus, she added, 'Yes, I'd like to dance.' She had vowed never to be afraid of any man again, and she was damned if she would allow Marcus to intimidate her.

The others left, and Eloise found herself held in Marcus's arms, moving around the dance floor to blues music in a state of nervous tension.

Marcus glanced down at her stiffly held head. The thick red coronet of curls had sprouted a few tendrils around her face. He could feel the tension in her and he deliberately tightened his hold, moving more heavily against her.

She shivered in response, but fought the emotion and won, by dint of squaring her shoulders and tilting back her head to stare up into his face. 'Are you going to tell me why, after three months of ignoring me, you've suddenly bought into our company?'

A satiric smile curved his expressive mouth. 'Perhaps I

saw a good deal, and took it,' he said smoothly. 'But you and I both know the real reason.'

'I have no idea,' she muttered, her eyes wide and puzzled, searched his hard features. Perhaps he wanted to make up to her for ignoring her past three months. The amazing thought popped into her head. It was an extravagant gesture, but maybe—just maybe—it was true, and for a while she allowed herself the luxury of believing it.

'No doubt you will enlighten me when you want to,' she said with the first genuine smile she had given him all evening. She was too confused and too tired to argue and, some of the tension easing out of her, she relaxed in his arms.

She knew damn well what he meant. Why else would she relax in his arms and smile? A ploy as old as Eve, but it was too little too late as far as Marcus was concerned. He knew it was a mockery of innocent surrender, but knowing that didn't lessen the impact of her sexy body against his. Marcus almost groaned out loud. Her softness seemed to accommodate the hard planes and angles of him as if made to measure. She was so beautiful, so sweet and receptive. *Christos!* Where had that come from? She was about as sweet as a wasp!

Reining in his raging libido, Marcus stopped and pushed her lightly away from him. He saw the surprise in her eyes, but ignored it. 'I think you and I need to talk, but not here, somewhere private.' Dropping a hand to her waist, he surveyed her beneath heavily hooded lids. 'My apartment or your hotel—take your pick.'

CHAPTER FIVE

SHE had been in danger in falling for his formidable charms all over again, Eloise thought with dismay. He only had to take her in his arms and every sensible thought flew her brain. *'Your place or mine.'* If he thought she was falling for that corny line, he was mistaken.

'Really, Marcus, surely you can come up with something better than that?' She gave a light laugh, casting him a glance from beneath the thick fringe of her lashes. 'I've heard better chat-up lines from a teenager.'

'I'm sure you have, and acted on them,' Marcus said, with dark emphasis. 'But, unlike Ted Charlton, I want a lot more from you than a one-night stand.'

'You think... Ted and me...?' Her sophistication slipped, and shock had her spluttering incoherently. 'Why, you...you...'

Grasping her by the elbow, he led her towards the table, his long fingers biting into the flesh of her arm as his dark head bent intimately towards her, giving the impression to anyone watching they were a close and loving couple, while mouthing harshly, 'You stole from my family.'

She was badly shaken by his assumption she had slept with Ted, and the instant racing of her pulse as his warm breath caressed her ear didn't help. She could barely take in what he was saying, until he concluded with sibilant softness, 'And I want you back in my bed until I consider the debt is paid.'

Involuntarily her jaw dropped. At the same time his hand fell from her arm and Eloise tilted her head to stare at him like a stranded trout, her mouth working and no sound coming out. Feeling the edge of a chair at the back of her knees, she collapsed down on the seat, and cast a panicked glance around the room. She was still in the nightclub, but she felt like Alice in Wonderland falling down the rabbit hole.

Come to think of it, the whole evening had been a bit like the Mad Hatter's tea party. And Marcus could certainly double as the Knave of Hearts, accusing *her* of sleeping with Ted Charlton, while he cut a swathe through women, she thought bitterly. She regarded him with wide angry eyes. And *stole* from him? As far she knew, he'd only been in business with them one day. Was he mad, or what?

'You're crazy,' she declared, finally finding her voice. 'You've completely lost your marbles.'

'No.' Marcus looked at her with cold contempt that made her skin crawl. 'I have the proof, Eloise. This time, you're not escaping the consequences of your actions. I'm going to make sure you don't.'

He was towering over like some great avenging angel— or devil was more apt, she corrected in her head. 'I have never stolen anything in my life. I have no idea what you are talking about,' she said, conviction in every syllable. 'I really don't.'

'Liar.' Marcus's cold eyes raked her with derision. 'You fell into my bed the last time we met, all wild and willing, simply to soften me up—and I nearly fell for it.'

She flinched as though she'd been struck. If only he knew the courage, the great leap of faith in his integrity it had taken for her to make love with him. If he'd continued their relationship, she might have confided in him by now, but she wasn't about to reveal her innermost fears to a man who had used her as a one-night stand.

And yet she could not explain to herself why it should hurt so much when Marcus looked at her with derision. She owed the man nothing.

Eloise opened her mouth, about to tell him so, but fear closed her throat as she recalled his other threat to have her back in his bed. Disgusted with herself, not Marcus, because for one heart-stopping moment she was tempted.

She had to get out of here! Picking up her purse, she tried to stand, but his hand on her shoulder forced her back down.

'Sit,' he ordered.

Eloise couldn't think straight, paralysed by shock as he pulled up a chair and sat beside her at the table, angling his seat so he could watch her every move. She felt sick inside, as with dawning horror she realised he actually believed what he was saying.

'You do well to remain silent.' Contemptuous amusement glittered in his dark eyes as he noted her bewilderment, the scarlet colour in her cheeks. 'Under that aura of innocence you wear so well beats the heart of a con-artist. A very talented, beautiful woman, but a thief nevertheless. I know what you are…' His glittering gaze rested on her with a blatant sexual intensity. 'And yet I want to possess that body, and until such time as I consider you have paid the debt you and your mother owe my family, you will stay with me.'

He had as good as called her a whore, but that paled into insignificance at the mention of her mother. A growing sense of dread seeped into Eloise's mind. 'What has my mother got to do with this?' she asked shakily.

'Oh, please!' Marcus mocked her supposed ignorance, but when she still stared at him with wary eyes, he gestured with his palms up. 'Okay, Eloise have it your way,' and he clarified with impatience, 'Chloe rented one of my uncle's villas, seduced the man, and then persuaded Theo to give her half a million to invest in her jewellery business—with your collusion, Eloise—and the pair of you vanished as soon as the cheque cleared.'

Appalled at the scenario Marcus presented, Eloise felt tension tighten her every muscle. Because, deep down, she had a horrible feeling there might be some truth in his words. Her mother had been close to Theo Toumbis when they'd stayed on Rykos. They'd departed in a hurry. Maybe Chloe had borrowed money from the man. Eloise had not known her mother well enough to say yes or no. But her mother was dead, and in deference to her memory at least deserved her support, Eloise staunchly reminded herself.

'You expect me to agree to be your, your mi—mistress.' She stammered over the word. 'Until I pay off some mythical debt I am supposed to owe you.' Eloise tried for a laugh. 'Dream on, Buster.' Pushing back her chair, she stood up again.

A chilling smile formed on his lips as he also rose to his feet 'Think about it. You agree to my terms, or I pull out of the deal with your firm.' His black eyes, gleaming with an unholy light of triumph, captured hers. 'Tonight's celebration, Eloise, will be looked on as a wake. Without the capital to maintain the Paris branch, you will have to close with a mountain of new debt, and within a very short space of time your London base will go bankrupt. I will make sure of it.'

'You can't do that!' Eloise gasped, amazed at the change in the man from sophisticated charmer into a ruthless, remote figure. She saw the implacable determination in his hard gaze, and she shook with fear and outrage. Rage won…

Well, he was not getting away with it. How dared he

threaten her like this? Who the hell did he think he was? 'I won't let you,' she snapped.

'You can't stop me,' Marcus said without a flicker of emotion. 'Speak to Harry—he will confirm what I say. I'll give you until tomorrow to decide. But think of the effect on Katy and Harry and their baby, their livelihood, before you make up your mind.' Dropping a bundle of notes on the table, he took her arm and urged her forward. 'This is too public.' His dark impervious gaze swept the room. 'Come on, I'll get you a cab,' he added smoothly, viewing her with dark threatening eyes.

'I don't need to think,' she spat, her fury rising to eclipse her earlier fear completely. 'The answer is no—and, as for Kate and Harry, they are my friends. They'll stand by me and ignore your ridiculous accusations.' Eloise took half a dozen enraged steps at his side without realising, then stopped suddenly, yanking her arm free.

'And I'll get my own cab,' she hissed. 'I want nothing from you, and this so-called business partnership will be dissolved tomorrow. I don't know how you talked Ted and Harry into it, but we are getting out.' She stepped out into the foyer.

'As you please.' Marcus's voice followed her, low and lethal. 'Then I will see you in court.'

The heated colour drained from her face. She stilled. The exit to the street and freedom was barely a step away, but for Eloise it might as well have been a million miles. Once she had given evidence in a court case, and it had been the worst experience of her life. No way could she face doing it again. Taking deep steadying breaths, she fought down the panic that threatened to choke her, and slowly turned to face Marcus. 'Court? What do you mean by court?' she demanded starkly.

'Unless we come to a private agreement, I shall of

course present the evidence of your deception to a court of law.' A shrug of his broad shoulders, and Marcus's mouth curled in a cynical smile, apparently registering a supreme masculine indifference either way that made her blood run cold. 'The decision is yours, but you no longer have until tomorrow. I want your answer tonight.'

Eloise swallowed hard, smoothed the fine fabric of her dress down over her hips with damp palms, and wondered what had happened to the Marcus she had first met. The Marcus who had valued her innocence, and then later the lover who had made her initiation into womanhood a magical experience. Was she really such a dim-wit that, for a few short hours, a few kind words and sweet caresses, she forgot what life had taught her? Men could be swine, and worse...

She would never make the same mistake again. Imperceptibly her shoulders straightened, and the ability to disguise her inner thoughts, developed with years of practice, slid back into place in her mind, like a steel trap door closing. She had vowed once never to trust another man as long as she lived, and for a brief space of time she had forgotten, but never again.

'What's it to be, Eloise?'

'First I want to see the so-called proof,' she demanded quietly and shivered at the cold implacability in his saturnine features.

'The evidence is at my apartment, ten minutes' drive away.' His arm closed firmly around her shoulders. 'We can continue this conversation better there, I'm sure you will agree.'

He had an apartment in Paris? Why not? A hysterical laugh fluttered in her throat. The man had everything. Marcus was a powerful, ruthless operator, a legend in the financial markets. Where lesser men made the occasional loss, what he had he kept, be it money, women or property. His nature was obviously possessive; he was a taker, not a giver.

But, held close to him, she could smell the faint musky masculine scent of him, and her traitorous skin heated where he touched. Dear heaven, if he did but know it, he could have had her and everything she was and owned for the asking three months ago—but not any more, she thought with the glimmer of an ironic smile as she agreed. She, more than most, did not appreciate being manipulated by a man—any man…

The apartment was small, more a pied-à-terre, tucked away at the top of one of the classic Napoleon-styled buildings overlooking the Seine. It was clearly designed with a bachelor in mind. A living room that was elegantly furnished and with what looked like a selection of original cartoons displayed on one wall, probably worth more than the apartment. A tiny kitchen area, obviously not meant to be used for anything other than making coffee or heating up a croissant for breakfast. A closed door led to what Marcus indicated was the bedroom, with an en-suite shower and toilet.

Eloise walked over to the ornate dormer window, and looked at the glittering lights reflected with the moonlight on the dark waters of the Seine, and wondered by what trick of fate she had ended up in this mess.

'Would you like a drink?' Marcus asked, standing much too close.

Eloise spun around. 'No. I want your so-called proof and an explanation fast,' she flashed back, disturbed by the intimacy of the place. 'It's not every day one is accused of being a thief.'

'So be it.' She watched as Marcus crossed to a desk in one corner. He opened a drawer, took out a folder, and placed it on the desk, and then laid a document on top. Switching on a desk lamp, he straightened up. 'Feel free to peruse them at your leisure,' he drawled mockingly. 'I need a drink.'

Eloise marched across to the desk, and picked up the document and read the first line. She raked a shaking hand through her hair forgetting her elaborate coronet of curls, in the process. It appeared to be a contract between Chloe Baker, her late mother, and Theo Toumbis, selling Theo a half share in Chloe's latest business venture in designer jewellery for five hundred thousand pounds—"Eloise By Design," to be situated in London.

Slowly, with mounting horror, she read on and there at the foot of the page were the three signatures to the contract: Chloe Baker, Theo Toumbis, and last Eloise Baker.

Eloise stared, transfixed. It was an excellent copy of her handwriting, but in fact it wasn't even her real surname.

'I never signed this.' She cast a wild look over her shoulder at Marcus. 'You must believe me, I have never seen it before. My name is *Smith*,' she cried.

'So, five years ago you were not masquerading as Chloe's sister, you were not on Rykos, and you know nothing about the contract?' he drawled sardonically. 'Please spare me the lies. I was *there*, remember?'

'No, yes—no.' Eloise glanced back down at the paper in her hand. 'Chloe must have forged my signature,' she murmured in stricken disbelief at her mother's deceit, and her heart sank as she realised the futility of trying to explain.

Marcus was right; she had been acting as Chloe's sister on the island. A good lawyer would make mincemeat of her claim to be innocent of any knowledge of the affair. She let the document flutter from her hand to the desk and in the process saw the blue folder.

'Oh, no!' she exclaimed, wide eyed with horror she stared at the folder. She knew exactly what it contained before she even opened it. But she made herself open it. She had to have her worst fear confirmed.

'Oh, yes, Eloise.' Marcus appeared at her side, and handed her a crystal glass. 'I think you might need this now,' he said with a grim smile.

She took the glass and took a hasty swallow. Brandy or whisky, she wasn't sure—but, coughing violently, she brushed past Marcus and slid down onto the sofa in a movement singularly lacking in grace. The glass clasped in her hand, every vestige of colour drained from her face, and not even the alcohol could replace it. How could her own mother have done that to her?

Not only had Chloe forged her signature on the contract, the folder contained a copy of the project Eloise had completed for college. The only difference was Chloe had named herself as architect of the plan instead of Eloise. It was a complex business plan including the costings and all the design work, publicity etc, in setting up Eloise By Design, aimed at the top end of the market. It had been Eloise's ambition and dream career. She had received top marks for the assignment.

Later, when Chloe had appeared and Eloise had rather shyly shown her prize-winning project to her mother, she'd been thrilled when for the first time in her life Chloe had taken an interest in what she was studying. Chloe had told her she was very talented, very clever, and she was very proud of her. Naturally, when her mother asked if she could keep it as a memento, Eloise had said yes.

She took another mouthful of the fiery spirit; she needed it. Never in a million years would it have crossed Eloise's mind that her mother would use her assignment as a means to get money out of a man. But, from the little she had seen, that appeared to be exactly what her mother had done. Reeling with shock and the cringing sense of shame and humiliation she felt at her mother's actions, she drained the glass in her hand.

The alcohol kicking in, Eloise leant back against the high-backed sofa, and closed her eyes for a second, the enormity of her mother's deception almost impossible to bear. Slowly she opened her eyes, and cast a covert look at Marcus beneath the shadow of her long lashes. He had shed his jacket and tie, and his shirt lay open at his tanned throat. He was leaning negligently against the fireplace, twirling a glass of whisky in one hand, as though he had not a care in the world.

Well, bully for him, she thought bitterly, aggression taking over from humiliation. Marcus was not getting away with blaming her. 'So my mother apparently conned your uncle into investing in a mythical company. Big deal! That was his mistake.' And she offered a grudging explanation, though she did not think the arrogant jerk deserved it. 'As for the business plan she used, yes, it was mine. My end of year's assignment at art college, nothing more. My mother kept it as a memento. But KHE is not the same company, and your uncle's problem has nothing to do with me,' Eloise declared defiantly and, picking up her purse, she stood up. 'And given they are both dead I very much doubt the dead can sue anyone,' she ended caustically.

He must take her for a prize fool. It hurt her deeply that her mother had used her idea, but that did not make Eloise responsible, and she'd never seen any of the money. Marcus had no case. She was calling his bluff...

'You should stick to designing, Eloise; your grasp of law is negligible. I am the executor of Theo's estate and as such can sue on behalf of his family,' Marcus informed her curtly, a dark gleam simmering like the threat of a lightning storm in the back of his fierce gaze. 'The name you were using at the time is on the contract. Eloise By Design or KHE, the intention and setting up of the company was the same. I also happen to know Theo's money ended up in a joint bank account between you and your mother. I also know you emptied the account to buy the London property you use for business.'

Eloise froze, her hand tightening in a death grip on her purse, her knuckles gleaming white with the strain. 'Oh, my God!' she gasped. She had forgotten all about the joint account. The account her mother had insisted on setting up supposedly to keep the money from the sale of the family home between them. The money Eloise had wanted to give her outright. The account Eloise had never touched until after her mother's death. She had been amazed at the amount of money her mother had left her. But, as her mother's lawyer had pointed out at the time, Chloe had been a very successful business woman.

But what kind of business—thieving? She had even stolen from her own daughter! There could be no doubt about it, Chloe had actually used Eloise's college project to con Theo Toumbis into thinking he was investing in a new company, and forged Eloise's signature...

Sadly Eloise realised she had never really known her mother at all. She had carried an idealised version of a brilliantly successful, elegant woman in her heart and mind for so long, the realisation it was all a myth was a brutal blow and her disillusionment was total.

'Waiting for divine intervention is not going to help you.' Marcus's mocking voice split the lengthening silence. 'You have two choices, my deal or the courts. So what is it to be?'

Little did he know Eloise thought bitterly, that there was no choice at all! She could not go to court...not after what had happened. She risked a glance at his rock-hard profile, the innate ruthlessness in every chiselled line, and any thought of pleading with him died a death. Not that she would have done that anyway, she immediately corrected. She had fought too long and hard for her pride and self-esteem to throw it away on a pig like Marcus.

Drawing on all her considerable will power, she slowly sat back down on the sofa. 'Why are you doing this?' She lifted glacial green eyes to his face. 'Why invest in a company you want to ruin?'

'Admittedly, that wasn't my first plan. Theo was a fool; he gave money to your mother at a time when he was expanding his holiday development on Rykos. It was money he could not afford, and for the next four years he struggled with a cash flow problem, but was too proud to ask for my help. He only mentioned the matter to me a week before he died when his company was going bankrupt.'

'Bankrupt.' Eloise almost groaned out loud; it was getting worse by the second.

'Obviously, as executor of his estate, it is my responsibility to make sure his wife and daughter do not suffer from his stupidity. Revenge is a totally human emotion, and, I admit, I went seeking it from your mother. It took some time for the detective agency I hired to track her down, only to discover she was dead, and there was no *sister*, only a daughter—it took a while longer to track you down,' Marcus declared harshly.

'But in memory of the innocent girl I once knew, I intended to give you the benefit of the doubt. I told myself you were young and probably influenced by your crooked mother. I checked you and KHE out and saw it was a quite profitable company with potential, and I was prepared to simply ask for Theo's investment back over time.'

He had remembered her, and he had been prepared to believe her. That went a long way to improving Eloise's view of him. 'That's a good idea,' she agreed, a glimmer of hope lighting her eyes for a moment. 'I'm sure we can come to some arrangement...'

'Oh, no, Eloise, that option has gone.' In two lithe strides he was standing over her. 'I was prepared to compromise my own convictions because I wanted you in my bed, to finish what we started five years ago. But not any more,' Marcus responded with silken softness. 'Not when I discovered after sharing my bed you quite happily admitted to having shared Ted Charlton's not twenty-four hours earlier, simply to get his money for your business,' he reminded her, his black eyes raking over her in utter contempt. 'You were obviously up to your old tricks again.'

'That's a lie,' Eloise gasped, so horrified by his unjust and ridiculous accusation she could only stare up at him.

'And I am supposed to believe you?' One dark brow arched sardonically. He watched every last scrap of colour slide from her cheeks. God, but she was good, he thought cynically, before adding, 'No way.'

Eloise leapt to her feet. 'You're wrong—I never slept with Ted! And you have a damn cheek insinuating I did,' she flung back at him, her temper simmering.

'Ted told me otherwise. He called me in New York and offered me his share in KHE. Apparently his ex-wife's lawyers had taken him to the cleaners, and he needed the money. It was an intriguing prospect and I helped Ted out of his problem, and acquired part of what should have been my uncle's anyway.'

'You did it to help Ted; how altruistic of you,' Eloise sneered, squashing the wayward thought that perhaps he had done it to help Ted out of a jam. Telling herself

Marcus was rich enough to buy a hundred companies without batting an eye.

'I thought so at the time, until we had a night out to celebrate clinching the deal, and Ted got quite drunk. Ted quite openly admitted to sleeping with you.'

'No, Ted wouldn't do that,' she cried.

'Yes, he did, and I was using sleep as an euphemism.' Marcus drawled sardonically 'We both know what you do in bed.'

Eloise reddened furiously. She had defended her honour once in front of a judge, and the experience had almost destroyed her. Never again.

'You bastard.' Her hand flung wildly and cracked against his olive skinned cheek. 'I have had enough of you,' she screamed, totally losing it. He had dragged up old memories—as if it wasn't enough to know her mother had betrayed her, but so had Ted and Marcus. She was distraught, fed-up and furious. Catching her wildly swinging hand, Marcus yanked her into his arms. She struggled desperately against his hard body. 'Let go of me,' she seethed.

'No.' Marcus lifted her off her feet with frightening ease and, landing on the sofa, he pinned her back against the cushioned arm. 'I am not letting you go,' and his mouth crashed down on hers.

He kissed her with a raw passion; a sexuality that was as savage as it was exciting. Eloise felt his hungry need through every cell in her body, and for a timeless moment she responded with a hot mindless urgency, until he lifted his head and reality kicked in.

Stretched out beside her, Marcus stared down at her, noting the flush of passion on her expressive face, his lustrous dark eyes gleaming with pure male satisfaction. 'The chemistry hasn't changed—you want me,' he challenged in a deep dark voice. 'And, even knowing what kind of woman you are, I still want you,' he admitted with a chilling smile slanting his sensuous lips. 'I bought out Ted because I don't want him around you. I don't want any man near you except me.'

'But why?' she cried. He didn't love her—it was just sex—and she tried to struggle, kicking out at him, but only succeeded in entwining her leg around one of his.

'I thought I made myself abundantly clear, but if you insist.' His upper torso loomed half over her, an imprisoning hand tightened around her waist, lifting, reinforcing the physical contact she was trying to avoid, while his other hand tangled in her hair, tipping her head up to his.

'I know you, sweetheart,' Marcus drawled sardonically. 'Let you out of my sight and you will sweet-talk some wealthy old man into giving you the money you need to pay off your debt. Ted's offer was opportune. I own a large chunk of your company and I can prevent that happening.' Her heart was pounding, her eyes wide open and trained on his darkly handsome face which was taut with anger and something else she could not fail to recognise. 'And no woman makes a fool of me twice,' he concluded curtly.

Winded by the ruthless speed with which he had subdued her, breathless and forced into an intimate awareness of his hard muscled body, all the fight went out of her. But she did try to deny his last assumption. 'No. I didn't...' But he didn't give her the chance.

'No more lies,' Marcus rasped, and he kissed her again.

He wasn't going to listen to her and, even if he did, he would never believe her, not with the proof overwhelmingly against her. His tongue hungrily probed the moist intimacy of her mouth. She wanted to resist, she really did... But a hoarse moan of capitulation was forced from her throat, and her taut body melted against him. She reached for his shoulders and kissed him back with help-less abandon.

The why and wherefore no longer mattered. Time had no meaning; all that existed was the miraculous world of delicious sensations, which only Marcus could provide. His hand at her back urged her up and the strapless bodice of her dress was somehow pushed down. His dark head lowered, burying his head in the soft swell of her breasts until his mouth found a taut nipple to suckle with fierce pleasure.

Three long months, and suddenly physical feelings that she had tried so desperately to suppress exploded in a fe-verish response. The blood flowed thick and hot through her veins. Her fingers spread up and out to bury in the silken depths of his black hair and hold him to her, never wanting the excitement to end.

Marcus lifted his head and looked down at her pale skin hectically flushed with the heat of arousal. 'You're mine,' Marcus grated roughly. 'For as long as I want you.' His glittering dark eyes clashed with her dazed green, and he smiled a predatory twist of his sensuous lips and, rearing back, shrugged off his shirt his hands going to the waist-band of his trousers.

Cool air washed over her aching breasts and a tiny voice of sanity echoed in her head. Her mouth ran suddenly dry, and she tensed in rejection at what she was inviting.

'No,' Eloise groaned. Whether she was decrying his abandonment of their lovemaking or denying him, she didn't actually know herself.

Marcus swore viciously under his breath. His dark eyes, leaping with anger, flashed to hers. 'No. You say no?' His hands stilled at his waist.

'Yes.' Suddenly she was afraid of the half-naked man looming over her.

He almost threw her away from him, her head bouncing on the arm of the sofa as he stood up, and stared down at her with icy eyes.

'You're a very sensual woman. Your whole body trembles when I touch you, your eyes flash emerald sparks, you want me—but obviously your stock in trade is to tease. Well, forget it with me... I've never forced a woman in my life, and I'm not about to start with you. I can't abide a tease.'

CHAPTER SIX

MARCUS could not have hurt her more if he had tried for a lifetime!

A flashback of another time—another man, equally as hard—calling her the same, and the eyes of every one in the courtroom fixed on her. She blinked rapidly and snapped out of her sensual daze. Sick with horror, Eloise stared at Marcus. He thought she was a tease, along with a thief and a whore, so why did her traitorous body react so excitedly with this one man, when he obviously despised her?

Suddenly she was plunged into complete turmoil between her thoughts and emotions. She was deeply ashamed of the fact that she could not withstand Marcus's particular brand of blatant sexuality, even though she knew he had no respect, no love for her at all.

Ashen-faced, she struggled into a sitting position, and pulled her dress up over her tight, aching breasts. Head bent, her hair cascaded either side of her face, hopefully masking the humiliation and desperation she felt from his too astute eyes. She clasped her hands in her lap, her fingers entwining nervously. Her heart raced and she fought for breath—panic or passion, she didn't know.

Marcus saw the pallor of her face before she hid it from him. He noted the defeated droop of her shoulders covered by the mass of her glorious red hair. She looked like some fragile, broken tiger lily sitting there.

Where the hell had that maudlin thought come from? He frowned and shoved his hands into the pocket of his trousers, willing his aroused flesh to subside. She was a man-eating tiger all right. The fragile flower act was a ploy to catch her prey, and he would do well to remember that. His frown deepened. 'What's it to be, Eloise?' A private arrangement or the courts?'

He might as well have said a private affair, because that was what he was demanding from her. She lifted her head. He was standing a foot away, his black hair ruffled where she had run her fingers through it, naked from the waist up. His bronzed torso glistened in the dim light, the muscles clearly defined. She thought of how he had kissed, of how it had felt to have his mouth at her breast, and wished he would put his shirt back on.

'Not the court,' she said a little unsteadily, lowering her eyes. Marcus couldn't possibly know and she couldn't tell him, but it had coloured her life for years.

It had been a sunny June evening, and a game of tennis on the public courts in the park with a student friend. Eloise at twenty had thought nothing of walking back across the park to the flat she shared with Katy. Until she was grabbed from behind, a horrible dirty hand squeezing her breast, and she was dragged into some bushes. Her attacker had had a knife, but she had screamed anyway and struggled like mad, lashing out with her tennis racket. Her top was ripped from her body, and the short tennis skirt was no barrier to the man's marauding hand. The knife was at her throat and she was giving up hope of escape when a dog pounced on her attacker. He lashed out with the knife and slashed her leg before running off. The man was caught, but as horrific as the attack had been the court case that followed was worse.

Eloise would never forget facing her attacker in court, nor could she forget the defence lawyer. He raped her with words. Her perfectly conventional tennis outfit became clothing designed to tease, a deliberate provocation. It was her fault she had long legs, long hair; she shared a flat with a man, the fact it was Katy's boyfriend ignored. The lawyer made her feel dirty and ashamed. The case took two days, and by the end of it when a guilty verdict was returned Eloise was too emotionally shattered to care. And she vowed she would never set foot in a court again.

Lifting her head, she stared at Marcus with cold green eyes. 'Definitely not the court.'

A cynical smile twisted Marcus's hard mouth. 'No court.' Why did that not surprise him? It simply confirmed she was guilty and she knew it. Still, what did he care for her morals or lack of them? He wanted her sinfully sexy body in his bed, until he sated himself, and she obviously knew the score, so there would be no messy break-up when he tired of her. His conscience clear, reaching out, he grasped her upper arms and hauled her to her feet.

'Instead, you agree to be my mistress for one year, *exclusively* mine,' he emphasised, his dark deep-set eyes burning into Eloise's. 'I don't share, understand?'

She understood, all right. One year in his bed: it was blackmail, pure and simple. Well, maybe not so pure…

'At the end of that time I will give you the evidence of the fraud and cancel your debt.'

'I would prefer to pay back the money my *mother* stole.' Eloise accented the word. 'Not me,' she added forcibly; she was not admitting a guilt she did not feel.

'That isn't an option.' But Marcus had to give her points for trying; she looked so defiant, her green eyes blazing, and infinitely desirable. He wondered if he should have said two, or maybe three years.

Realistically, she knew if she lived as poor as a church mouse it would take her years to pay back the money, unless she sold the house, and that would ruin her relationship with her friends, never mind what it would do to the business. It was a catch twenty-two situation. She looked into his hard dark eyes, and she knew he would carry out his threat of court action.

A tiny shiver slivered down her spine, and suddenly she was fiercely aware of his long fingers on the flesh of her upper arms, the sensual heat emanating from his hard body. She thought of his lovemaking; the experience had been an earth-shattering, life-changing experience for her. But how did she know what it had been for him? Not love, that was for sure, but good enough sex as he wanted more, she realised grimly. As for what she wanted, her body had already answered for her, her nipples tight against the bodice of her dress.

'All right,' Eloise said lowering her eyes from his to intense gaze, afraid he would see more than she wanted him to know. 'I agree, one year from today and we go our separate ways.'

'I knew you would be sensible, after all what have you got to lose?' he husked, his hands stroking up over the soft curve of her shoulders.

Eloise didn't answer for a long moment. *I knew you would be sensible.* His arrogant assumption stiffened her spine, as nothing else could have done, a slow-growing, icy anger invading every cell in her body. Marcus did not know her at all, and never would...

For four years she had had no faith in her own femininity and had repressed all her sexual urges, until three months ago when Marcus had shown her in one memorable night what it was to be a woman. For a while she had confused lust with love. But by not contacting her again Marcus had effectively disabused her of the notion, and his actions tonight simply underlined the point.

For the first time in her life she faced up to the fact she

was a mature woman, a sensual being with needs and desires of her own and she had no need to be ashamed of them… Ironically, Marcus had taught her that tonight as well. If sex was all he wanted, *what had she got to lose?* His words! They had already been lovers, and she did want him; she had a sneaky suspicion he might be the only man she wanted. But she owed him no loyalty, nothing, and she could walk away when the time came with her business and life intact.

She let her gaze slide over him, sizing him up, tall powerful, authority stamped in every line, a pure alpha male. She didn't doubt he would take her to court. She lifted her eyes to his face—strikingly handsome, with a strong jaw that was beginning to show a dark shadow, and a wickedly sensuous mouth—and she had made her decision. Why not use him as he intended using her?

'Nothing. Nothing at all,' she finally answered. Eloise saw the blaze of triumph in the glittering depths of his eyes, and his satisfied smile. She felt his hand tighten on her shoulder. She knew he was going to kiss her and she waited until his dark head bent towards her before tilting up her chin determinedly and meeting his smile with a cold one of her own.

'But first we will have to work out the technicalities,' she said brusquely, and saw his head lift and the flicker of surprise chase across his handsome features. 'I will not have Katy or Harry involved in any way in our private arrangement.'

Marcus couldn't read the expression in the depths of her huge emerald eyes. But he guessed she was thinking there was really no way out for her. And this was her way of gaining some kind of control.

'I agree, strictly personal between you and I.' He could be magnanimous in victory, and let her think she had won a point. He drew her closer, he had more pressing needs right at this moment. 'After all it isn't Katy or Harry I want to sleep with,' Marcus drawled in a deep husky tone, his breath fanning her cheek.

She had agreed to be his for one year. He should have felt elated but he couldn't help wondering what her eyes would look like if they were shining with joy for the man she loved, instead of the man she had agreed to sleep with for money, because the bottom line was, that was what she'd just done.

For a second his fingers dug almost angrily into the tender flesh of her shoulder, refusing to admit he was disappointed, telling himself revenge was sweet.

'Marcus…' Eloise planted her hands on his chest with the intention of holding him away. Immediately she knew it was a mistake; the hot heat of his skin beneath her palms was an enticement to stroke, to linger, to explore the muscular contours.

'I love the way you say my name,' he declared throatily. His dark head lowered and his carnal mouth found her parted lips.

The instant their mouths met, Eloise sank beneath a hot hungry surge of passion. It shouldn't be like this, but it was what she'd just agreed their arrangement should be, and her treacherous body felt otherwise. She surrendered instantly to the drugging pleasure of his sensuous mouth and the heated caress of his hands, and within seconds constructive thought became impossible.

His hands wrenched down the top of her strapless dress again, and with a groan Marcus lifted her and suckled an erect rosy nipple. It was a torment, a sweet torment that sent quivering need lancing through her body, and a shocked cry escaped her convulsed throat.

Somehow she was on her back on the sofa, with Marcus

on top of her. He skated a hand over her burgeoning breast, his dark eyes blazing down at her, as his long fingers toyed with her sensitised flesh until she was utterly possessed by the power of sensation. Her hands clasped his broad, tanned shoulders, her fingers trailed with tactile delight over the satin-smooth skin to tangle in the soft curling chest hair, scratching a hard male nipple.

With a low groan Marcus's dark head dipped, and his mouth was on her breast again, but this time his tongue and teeth sent her shuddering into spasm after spasm of mindless pleasure. She twisted urgently beneath him, possessed by a need, a hunger so intense she was lost to all else.

Sinking back on his knees, Marcus grated, 'I want you now,' and a large hand skimmed the fabric of her gown down over her hips and legs, and tossed it to the ground. 'Damn it, I can't wait!' His eyes black pools of desire in the taut planes of his face, he stared down at her. His long elegant fingers grasped the tiny black lace briefs, her only covering, and drew them from her body.

Naked beneath him, Eloise didn't care. He was hot and hard and very male, and she was amazed at her own pleasure in simply looking. But looking was not enough; she wanted him naked as herself. Involuntarily, she reached out her hand and fumbled with the fastening of his trousers. He did it for her...

With a low laugh, a husky sound of primitive pleasure, Marcus covered her mouth with rough drugging kisses, as he dispensed with the remainder of his clothes.

He reared over her, naked, and without warning, in an explosion of renewed passion, he kissed his way down her sensitised body, mouth, breasts, stomach, and finally settled at the juncture of her thighs.

She arched off the sofa like an arrow from a bow, shuddering uncontrollably; never had she experienced such intimacy. She tangled her fingers in the night-black hair of his head, and urged him back up to her.

'You drive me mad.' Marcus growled when he drew level with her passion-glazed face.

He took her swollen mouth with a raw, savage hunger that sent her over the edge into a wild writhing wanton in his arms. She rubbed her aching breasts against his chest. Her arms wrapped around his neck, her fingers digging into his flesh. His hands swept down her body in one long, heated caress and then he lifted her, curling her legs around his lean waist, and surged into her in one mighty thrust.

Stilling for a moment, he shuddered against her, his molten black eyes almost angry burning into hers. 'You do this to me,' he rasped, and thrust again.

Eloise felt him move with every pore and cell in her body, smooth and slow, then fast and rough, driving her ever higher until she was consumed by the mighty primeval rhythm of his huge body, the explosive force of his virility urging her to the ultimate peak of excitement. She sank her teeth into his shoulder, as she soared over the edge into a clenching quivering climax at the same time as he did.

Pinned beneath him, and shivering in the aftermath of passion, Eloise tried to get her tumultuous emotions under some kind of control. But all she could think of was the blessed weight of his hot, damp body, his heartbeat thumping against her breast, the heavy sound of his laboured breathing, a symphony to her ears. Her hands stroked down his broad back, loving the sensation of sweat-slicked skin beneath her fingers, loving him... No... She must not confuse great sex with anything else, ever again. She meant nothing to him, and when he abruptly rolled off her and stood up, she told herself she was glad, burying the memory of the afterglow of pleasure they had shared the first time they had made love in the deepest recess of her mind. She wanted nothing from Marcus, no emotional involvement of any kind, she ruled in her head.

She glanced up at Marcus and was suddenly extremely conscious of her naked state, but it was obvious he didn't feel as awkward as she did. With casual ease he picked up his trousers and stepped into them, zipped the fly, and just as casually bent and picked up her dress and dropped it on her.

'Cover yourself. You don't want to catch cold.'

Catch cold? He had to be joking! She had burned for him, and even now simply looking at him brought warmth to her face she could not hide.

But he wasn't joking. His dark eyes raked over her in analytical scrutiny, and he concluded. 'You're incredibly beautiful, incredibly sexy, but with no morals. Still, two out of three isn't bad,' he offered with a husky laugh. 'There is a bed next door.' A smile curved his sexy mouth, his dark eyes gleaming with renewed desire. 'Let's use it.'

'Let's not.' Eloise pulled her dress over her head and stood up, smoothing the fabric over her slender hips. His amusement and obvious contempt for her as an individual was enough to re-enforce her *no emotional involvement* rule. Marcus hated her, and yet she had fallen into his arms like a ripe plum, and loved every second, she admitted honestly. But she had no intention of following his every command like some concubine; her pride would not let her.

Why, why Marcus? How was it Marcus could turn her into a weak, needy woman, when other men, even men she knew well and respected, left her cold? It had to be her own traumatic past. Plus, she dryly admitted, his undoubted sexual expertise had made her a victim to her own body's uncontrollable desire for the man, and she didn't want to be. She was no man's victim.

With that thought uppermost in her mind, she raked her hands through the tumbled mass of her hair and, discovering a couple of hair pins, she twisted her hair into a knot at her nape, fixed with the pins. Making a determined effort to appear sophisticated, she straightened up and directed a cool glance at Marcus.

'I have to leave. I have a breakfast meeting with Katy and Harry and, as we agreed, it's better they know nothing about...' Was it an affair? Business. She struggled with the wording, the colour rising in her cheeks. 'Our arrangement,' she finally settled on.

'Our arrangement,' Marcus drawled with a sardonic arch of one dark brow. She was doing it again, blushing... The little witch actually thought he was going to sneak around like some illicit lover. Well, she was in for a rude awakening.

'I think the word you are looking for is *affair*, Eloise, and as for keeping it a secret—' he gave her a chilling half-smile '—forget it. You and I are partners in every way, and I will attend the breakfast meeting with you.'

The horrible part was, Eloise knew she could not stop him. Her gaze slid over his half naked body, igniting a familiar flare of heat deep inside her, and she tried to dampen it down. 'With your investment in KHE, that is your prerogative.' She endeavoured to keep the conversation impersonal. But how could her voice sound so matter-of-fact, when inside she was a mass of confusing emotions? she wondered.

'Yes, and don't you forget it.' Black eyes glittered over her taut figure. 'We are going to have a very public affair, Eloise. As I told you before, I'm not taking the chance of you finding some other wealthy fool to bail you out.'

Eloise looked at him, incredulous and inexplicably hurt. 'You imagine I would do that?'

'I know so.' He gave a sardonic laugh. 'And I see no reason to take an unnecessary risk. You will be publicly labelled Kouvaris's woman.' Broad shoulders lifted in a casual shrug. 'I have yet to meet a man brave enough to cross me.' His firm lips curved at the corners in a cynical smile. 'Or foolish enough.'

It was the supreme arrogance that got to Eloise. Her palm itched and she longed to smack the grin off his face, but warring emotions stayed her hand. She did not dare, if she hoped to persuade him to at least try and be discreet. Her stomach churned over at the thought of being branded Marcus's woman. She cherished her privacy above everything.

She looked at him, her green eyes colliding with hard black, and it took every ounce of will power she possessed to hold his gaze. 'Katy knows me well. She will never believe we are an item, not so fast,' she said softly.

Marcus threw his head back and laughed out loud and, taking a step forward, his hands settled on her shoulders. 'Eloise.' He shook his dark head, his eyes lit with amusement roamed over her. 'But we were sweethearts on our first dinner date,' he declared with shattering logic. 'I bet the last three months you waited for my call, wondered where I was and with whom. And tonight, as soon as you saw me, your gorgeous eyes dilated, and that sexy body of yours sent off signals like the firing of a rocket on the launch pad.'

Mortified, Eloise swallowed hard. 'That's not true,' she muttered.

'Katy might know your mind, but your body is all mine. Do you want me to prove it to you again?' Marcus said softly into the suddenly tension-filled atmosphere.

'No.' Her green eyes pleaded with him. 'But please will you be discreet in front of Katy and Harry, at least until they leave Paris? I'll think of something to tell Katy when I get home.' Her lips thinned. 'Obviously not the truth.'

'Yes, okay.' Marcus was prepared to set her mind at rest for the moment.

'Thank you,' Eloise managed to say and, taking a step back, she added, 'You can call me that cab now.' And, while she waited for the taxi, she told him the name of the hotel and the time of the breakfast meeting, plus some of her latest ideas.

Marcus looked at Eloise. She had backed away from him, as far as the door, as if she could not get away fast enough. She was rambling on, and he was pretty sure, she had no idea what she was talking about. As he watched, he realised she actually was incredibly nervous, if not frightened.

His gut tightened, and for a second he wondered if she really was afraid of him, but then he saw the tip of her tongue lick over her bottom lip, swollen from the passion of their kisses. Hell, no, she had wanted him every bit as he wanted her. He was falling into the same old trap of assigning finer feelings to the woman, when he knew for a fact she did not have any. It was more likely she did not want her friend Katy to discover the dubious deal she and her mother had got up to, and realise that Eloise was not quite the honest, straightforward girl she appeared to be.

Picking up his shirt, he slipped it on, a smug smile curving his mouth as Eloise was silenced for a moment, her green eyes watching his every move with a fascination she had great difficulty disguising. He stepped towards her.

The entry phone pealed. The cab had arrived.

Marcus took her down to the street. The soft light of the street lamp turned her glorious red hair into a fiery halo, and he couldn't help himself. He clasped her face between his hands and looked deep into her emerald eyes, then bent his head and kissed her gently on her softly swollen lips. He felt the sudden tremor sweep through her and her sudden tension as she tried to prevent her reaction.

Her resistance was a challenge and he was about to deepen the kiss, show her the futility of trying to deny the devastating physical desire between them. But for some inexplicable reason he didn't. 'I'll see you back to your hotel,' he offered softly, running an elegant finger down the soft curve of her cheek, before setting her free. 'If you like.' He gave her the choice.

'No. No, thanks. We will meet at breakfast in a few hours.'

Once inside her hotel room, Eloise headed straight for the shower. She stood under the powerful spray, scrubbing at her slender body, trying to remove the scent of Marcus from her skin. But it was a futile exercise. She only had to think of him to taste him on her tongue, feel him on her skin, and after five minutes she gave up. Drying herself down with a large fluffy towel, she walked back into the bedroom and, picking up the white cotton tee-shirt she favoured for sleeping in, slipped between the sheets on the wide bed and closed her eyes.

But sleep was a long time in coming. She could have spent the night lying in Marcus's arms. A tear trickled from the corner of her eyes to flow smoothly down her cheek. No matter how she tried to pretend, she knew in her heart she could easily fall in love with Marcus all over again. In his arms she felt safe and loved, which in reality was stupid, she knew. There was no denying the power of the sexual chemistry between them, but it could not negate the fact that they didn't even like each other. He thought she was a thief and worse. Her innate honesty forced her to admit he had good reason to think so. But did that justify his treatment of her? She had tried to explain but he was incapable of listening, or only heard what he wanted to hear.

She had met a lawyer like that in the criminal court at the tender age of twenty, and it had taken her years to recover from the verbal mauling. Consequently, she was not prepared to justify herself to any man ever again.

No, she would play his game, act the worldly woman he imagined she was until his desire for revenge on her ran out. Dear heaven, she'd had plenty of practice at hiding her true emotions. As a child she'd pretended to her grandparents and everyone else she didn't mind her parents never being around. How hard could it be to act the successful, sophisticated mistress of a man like Marcus for one solitary year? A vivid mental image of his glorious naked body filled her mind. Not hard at all when the fringe benefits were spectacular sex, she thought, her temperature rising. She rolled over onto her stomach, muffling a groan of frustration in the pillow, and finally fell asleep.

CHAPTER SEVEN

AT SEVEN-THIRTY the next morning Eloise walked into the dining room of the hotel. She had dressed with care in slim-fitting stone linen trousers, with a matching jacket and mint-green silk top beneath. With the careful use of cosmetics, she hoped she had disguised the ravages of the emotional turmoil and sleepless night from her friends' view. She needn't have worried! A glimmer of a smile curved her full lips as she saw Katy and Harry already seated at a table, by a window overlooking the river. Katy was wearing sunglasses.

Eloise walked over and joined them. 'Hangover, Katy?' she prompted, pulling out a chair and slipping off her jacket. She placed it around the back and sat down opposite her friends.

'And good morning to you, too,' Katy mocked, and Harry laughed.

'Got it in one, Eloise. My wife's first big night out since becoming a mum, and she has overdone it somewhat. Poor Floe got up with the baby during the night, and she's busy packing for all of us. Help yourself to coffee, and you and I can run over what needs to be done. We'll save the big discussion until you return to England.' He cast a loving look to his wife. 'Katy is in no state to have any valid opinion on anything, this morning.'

Eloise poured herself a cup of coffee from the pot provided. The table was set for three and Harry had already ordered continental breakfast. She knew they were leaving for the airport by eight-thirty, and she felt a tiny stab of guilt because she had told Marcus the meeting was at eight-forty-five—but then, as she reminded herself, she didn't owe him any loyalty.

Katy groaned. 'You're right. Keep it light.' Removing her sunglasses, she winced. 'My God, never again!' And, raising bleary eyes to Eloise, she added, 'Trust you to look good. So come on, tell me what you and our new partner Marcus got up to last night after we left?'

'We had a dance and I got a cab home.' Eloise took a long swallow of her coffee, successfully fighting back the blush that threatened. She had a vital question of her own she wanted answered. She had realised in the early hours before dawn when she had time to think straight, Marcus couldn't have blackmailed her half as effectively if he had not now owned a chunk of their company.

Eloise was no fool. She'd realised if it had been a simple question of repaying the money her mother stole, she could probably have arranged a loan on the property that housed the company. It was in her name but was rented at a pep-percorn rent to KHE. Unfortunately, with Marcus now having taken over Ted Charlton's investment in KHE and added a considerable amount to it, he was in a position to ruin them. She didn't trust him an inch, and the more she thought about it the more she did not believe Marcus had bought Ted's share in KHE simply to help the man out. It would not surprise her at all to discover it was the other way around. Marcus had sought Ted out to get a bigger hold over Eloise. He obviously had a healthy appetite for revenge.

'I want to talk to you about Marcus.' Her determined green eyes fixed on Harry. 'How exactly did he become involved with our business? I do think you should have discussed it with me first.' She didn't want to fall out with

Harry, but she could not allow the unorthodox way Harry had behaved go unchallenged.

For the next few minutes Harry explained and, by the time he'd finished, even Eloise could see there was nothing much else he could have done. Apparently Ted Charlton had informed Harry a few weeks ago his divorce settlement had cost more than he thought, and he was going to have to pull out of the deal. But Ted had called back a few days later and told him not to worry, he had lined up another backer, Mr Kouvaris, and he was prepared to invest twice as much as originally agreed. Harry hadn't wanted to worry Katy and Eloise, so he'd decided to keep it to himself until it was finalised and the Paris boutique opened.

Eloise could not argue with his reasoning. Harry had confirmed what Marcus had told her, that Ted had actually offered him the shares. Her sinister reading of the situation was wrong; her paranoia was showing again, she thought grimly.

Marcus had told her the truth, and it made her feel slightly better. But if she ever saw Ted Charlton again she had a few very pointed questions to ask him. Not least why he had told Marcus she had slept with him?

For the next half-hour they discussed the opening and various other matters, and it was suggested Eloise should stay in Paris for a week, rather than the couple of days first arranged, just to make sure everything was going smoothly.

'Okay.' Eloise agreed, draining her coffee after eating the last crumb of a particularly delicious chocolate croissant. 'But hadn't you two better collect Benjamin and Floe? You don't want to miss your flight.' She wanted them long gone before Marcus turned up.

Her stomach was churning and her palms were damp

just at the thought of Marcus's impending arrival. Eloise had little faith in her ability to pretend normality with Marcus in front of Katy. Her friend knew her too well, and she breathed an inward sigh of relief as Katy and Harry got to their feet. Shoving back her chair, she slipped her jacket off the back and stood up.

But her relief was short-lived.

'Well, good morning,' Katy exclaimed.

Eloise felt the hairs on the back of her neck stand on end and saw the smile on Katy's face, just before a strong male arm wrapped around her waist and drew her back into disturbing proximity with every elegant line of a large muscular body. Marcus was early!

'Good morning Katy, Harry,' Marcus intoned brightly.

Eloise stiffened, and shot him a startled glance. He looked vibrantly masculine, dressed casually in cream cotton pants and a matching polo shirt, his dark features relaxed in a broad smile—while tension knotted every muscle in her body, as she fought the tingling awareness his touch always invoked.

Feeling manipulated, but unable to do anything about it, she watched, as with a swift scrutiny of the remains of breakfast on the table Marcus remarked, 'I appear to be rather late.' His glittering gaze switched to her, and without warning his dark head swooped down, his firm lips brushing hers in a brief kiss. 'Eloise, darling, I thought you said eight forty-five. But I forgive you. It is such a delight to see you looking so beautiful and fresh after our late night.' With arrogant aggression his dark eyes lingered on her now scarlet face, challenging her to object to the intimacy.

The swine was doing it deliberately, Eloise thought furiously. So much for being discreet. She cast a glance at her friend and saw the look of astonishment on Katy's face. 'I must have made a mistake,' she muttered, trying to wriggle free from his restraining arm, but his fingers simply dug deeper into her waist.

'What late night, Eloise? You said you had a dance and caught a cab,' Katy demanded, but her eyes were smiling.

Marcus answered for her. 'She did…eventually. But only after we had visited a local place,' Marcus positively purred, as he surveyed Eloise with dark slumberous eyes, making no attempt to disguise the gleaming awareness in their depths. 'It was great, wasn't it, Eloise?' and he smiled.

She cast him a withering glance, and saw the wicked amusement in his smile. His apartment, local place—my eye! Eloise simmered with anger but, with her two friends watching, she could do nothing but agree. 'Yes.'

'Well, sorry you missed breakfast, Marcus,' Harry cut in. 'But we do have to dash. Not to worry, though, Eloise is staying the rest of the week, and she can fill you in on anything you need to know.'

'I'm sure she can,' Marcus drawled, with a long lingering look at Eloise.

Katy's gaze flicked between Eloise and the man holding her, a frown pleating her brow. 'It's okay, Harry, you stay and have a coffee with Marcus. Eloise can come upstairs and help me. I know she wants to say goodbye to her favourite godson,' she informed. 'We will meet you down here in twenty minutes.'

Marcus had to let Eloise go. But not before he had deliberately dropped another kiss on the top of her head with a murmured, 'Don't be long.'

'Right! What is going on?' Katy demanded as soon as they got in the elevator. 'Marcus is all over you like a rash, and I've never seen you so flustered.' She appraised Eloise with sharp eyes. 'Three months ago you had a dinner date with him and told me it was nothing, a meeting between old friends. Now the man is our partner and he can't keep his hands off you.'

Thankful for her escape from the blasted man for a while, Eloise looked into the slightly worried eyes of Katy. Her friend knew her past history far too well to be fooled into thinking Eloise would indulge in a casual affair, and she knew what she had to do.

'I think I'm in love.' She saw Katy's mouth fall open in shock. 'And I think Marcus feels the same.' Katy knew her too well to believe anything less. She had been Eloise's rock and support after the savage attack she'd suffered, and all through the horror of the court case and publicity that followed. She knew Eloise had never looked at a man since. But Katy was a romantic and Eloise knew nothing less than true love would do for Katy to believe her.

'And have you two, last night…well, I mean, did you?'

'Yes and it was fine,' Eloise said telling the truth at least partially, with a scarlet face.

'Oh, Eloise, I am so happy for you.' And suddenly Eloise was wrapped in Katy's arms. 'I knew one day everything would work out for you.'

Watching the happy family group bundle into the waiting cab, and drive away, all the energy drained out of Eloise. She had done it. She'd smiled and convinced Katy she was happy in her new relationship with Marcus. She'd listened while Katy had fantasised of course Marcus must have loved her all along, and that was why he'd invested in their small company. He'd done it for Eloise.

Eloise did not disillusion her, though it did cross her mind for one mad moment to tell Katy the truth, as they were all leaving and she was struck with the most horrendous feeling of being deserted. The safe, successful world she had built for herself was never going to be the same again. But hugging baby Benjamin to her breast and kissing him goodbye had convinced her she couldn't. There was no way on earth she would jeopardise Katy's happy family unit.

Pale and strained, she threw a bitterly resentful glance at Marcus. 'You certainly didn't waste any time publicising our sordid affair.' He'd turned and was walking back towards the bank of elevators on one wall, his hand apparently glued to her waist, urging her along. 'If you think your behaviour this morning was being discreet, then God help me.'

'Smile,' Marcus suggested silkily, his dark eyes absorbing the tense pallor of her beautiful face. 'Or people might think we're fighting.'

'Since when did you care what other people think?' she flung back, her nostrils flaring at the disturbingly familiar scent of him as he ushered her into the elevator and wrapped his arms around her. Stiff as a board, she glared up at him. 'You promised we would keep it private until they had left Paris.'

'So I lied. A man will promise anything to a woman to get her into bed. You are not that naïve, Eloise,' he opined sardonically. 'You've done the same yourself countless times, I have no doubt.' He shrugged his broad shoulders. 'After all, you lied to me about the time of the breakfast meeting.'

She went from red to as white as death. Being caught out in a lie was embarrassing, but realising he thought her capable of using her body to get what she wanted and it didn't actually bother him told her how little he truly thought of her. Anger and humiliation turned her stomach and she tore herself free from his restraining hold just as the elevator stopped.

'You slimy snake, why don't you take a hike?' she spat and, marching straight to her room, she slid the card in the lock and pushed the door. Nothing happened!

A flash of anger stayed Marcus's step for a moment. He was not in the habit of taking insults from a lady, and certainly not one he had thoroughly bedded only hours earlier. But then, she was no lady, he reminded himself. A liar—yes, and a very sexy one at that, and not worth getting angry over. But with a great rear, he thought as he followed her down the hallway. He wanted her in his bed, nothing more he told himself.

Marcus watched her futile attempt to open the door. Her face was pink, she was angry; no, angry didn't cut it. From the set of her jaw and the tension in every inch of her luscious body, he realised she was nervous, her small hand shaking.

'Allow me.' Marcus took the card from her trembling fingers, and opened the door and followed her inside.

'I told you to go.' Eloise turned on him.

Marcus reached out and held her by the shoulders. 'Is that really what you want?' His brown eyes darkened as they skimmed over her, lingering on the swift rise and fall of her breasts, clearly discernible beneath the fine silk blouse she wore, before returning to her face. He caught a brief glimpse of something very much like fear in her gorgeous green eyes, and inexplicably he felt a twinge of guilt.

He'd accused her of being a thief, and with all the subtlety of a tank he'd told her he wanted her in his bed. Then, while she was still trying to come to terms with the passion they'd shared last night, he'd strolled in on her this morning. Angry at her lie about the time, he'd deliberately embarrassed her in front of her friends, making it plain they were an item.

'Why don't we both take a hike, as you so eloquently put it?' Marcus prompted with a wry smile. 'We could spend the day sight-seeing, having fun.' He looked into her eyes, saw the angry puzzlement there, and felt a pang of conscience, but not enough to stop him drawing her against him and covering her mouth with his own.

'Stop it,' Eloise gasped. She fought him at first, twisting her head from side to side. But he was so persistent and oddly tender; his mouth moved gently against hers, not stopping until, with a little moan, she surrendered and kissed him back.

Marcus broke the kiss, put his hand under her chin, and tilted her head back. 'Spend the day with me.' Amused dark eyes rested assessingly on her beautiful if flushed face. 'You know you want to.'

She did... But catching the hint of mockery in his expression was enough to bring her back to reality with a bump.

'I have to go to work.' Jerkily, Eloise pulled away from him. 'That's why I am here.' And, crossing to the bed, she picked up her purse from the bedside cabinet. Once out of his reach, she took a few deep steadying breaths, managed to get her racing pulse under control and recovered some of her formidable strength of will. Turning, she tossed her head, her red hair flying around her lovely face, determination in every taut line of her slender body.

'After all, you do have an interest now in KHE, and the harder I work the more profit for you,' she said curtly.

Marcus gave a sardonic laugh. 'I'm glad you realise that,' he mocked. 'But, as I'm the boss in this affair, I decide which tasks you perform first.' He cast a provocative glance at the bed before his dark gaze returned to her shocked green.

The implication in his hooded eyes as she took a step

in the direction of the door filled her with disgust and, to her shame, a secret thrill. Her heartbeat leapt at the thickening of the atmosphere; fingers clutching her purse, she stepped hurriedly past him. 'I have to go... I have an appointment with the new sales assistant.'

'I'll come with you.'

Sharply disconcerted, she swung back around, and collided with gleaming black eyes. 'You, but...'

'As you so succinctly pointed out, I have a vested interest in the business.'

Two hours later, Eloise walked out of their new shop, silently fuming. She'd thought she was doing quite well with her schoolgirl French, explaining to the new manageress—a very elegant French lady—and a younger female assistant what was expected of them. Then Marcus had cut in and introduced himself as a partner and wouldn't you just know it? Eloise thought, simmering with resentment. The man spoke fluent French, and charmed the two women so completely Eloise might as well not have been there, for all the notice they took of her.

'Did you have to be so damned interfering?' Eloise snapped, as they stood on the pavement in the summer sunshine. 'I'm perfectly capable of instructing the staff. You didn't have to fawn all over the women.'

Marcus caught the anger in her emerald eyes. A hectic flush coloured her cheeks, and he let his eyes wander with sensual intensity over her, lingering deliberately on the proud thrust of her breasts against the silk shirt. His sensuous mouth quirked at the corners in a knowing grin and he chuckled.

She felt her nipples tighten, and his chuckle simply enraged her further. 'What's so funny?' she snarled.

Throwing an arm around her stiff shoulders, he drew her into his side. 'You're jealous, Eloise.'

It wasn't what Eloise had expected, and she spluttered, 'I am not, you egotistical baboon!'

After a second's pause Marcus threw his dark head back and laughed out loud. 'Well, I suppose a baboon is a step up from a snake. But you are jealous?' His amusement lingered in the narrowed eyes that studied her face. He brushed back a stray tendril of red hair curving her cheekbone. 'Why not admit the truth, Eloise?' he demanded huskily. 'It's the same for me.'

Marcus knew as soon as he said it, he had made a mistake. The man he had been five years ago when they first met, and he had thought her innocent, might have admitted to jealousy. But not the man he was today, with the evidence of her perfidiousness always at the back of his mind. He prided himself on being a sophisticated lover who delighted in women, and always brought them pleasure, but never, ever lost control or revealed his own emotions. Somehow Eloise had the damnable ability to make him forget what she really was, and he didn't like it.

What the hell? he told himself. For one day he was going to forget everything and just enjoy...

Eloise's heart skipped a beat. Marcus, jealous? The notion was balm to her battered pride and she was wretchedly aware of how much she wanted to believe him.

His dark head bent and he kissed her briefly on her lips. His arm dropped from her shoulders and he waved his hand in an expansive arc.

'Look around you, Eloise. The sun is shining, we are in Paris, a city designed for lovers and, whatever else is between us, we are lovers. Indulge me and let me show you around.'

She looked at him. The dark vitality of his masculinity was a potent temptation to any woman, and she was no exception. Why he wanted her didn't seem that important all of a sudden. The sun gilded his black hair in golden highlights. Eloise's admiring emerald eyes clashed with smouldering black, and his starkly handsome features darkened, a slow sensual smile curving his beautiful mouth. Her heart missed a beat and resumed at a faster pace.

He extended an elegant tanned hand towards her. 'Go with the flow, Eloise. Isn't that your English expression?' His accent thickened in his husky-voiced question and she allowed him to tuck her slender hand in his.

'Yes.' His glittering gaze mesmerised her. 'Yes, it is,' she agreed, and felt the flow of electricity from his touch through every nerve in her body.

'I thought the Eiffel Tower first. You agree.'

'Do I have a choice?' she prompted with a wry smile, seeing the determination in his expression. He really did mean to do the whole tourist bit, and somehow she found it rather endearing.

'For a beautiful lady, you ask far too many questions,' Marcus remarked and tugged her along the pavement.

They rode the elevator to the top of the Eiffel Tower. Eloise took one look at the panoramic view, and immediately her legs shook and her head spun. She saw Marcus gesture to something in the distance and vaguely heard his voice extolling the virtues of some building, but she felt dizzy. Reaching out, she gripped his arm, and clung. Heights were not her thing.

'Eloise.' His narrowed gaze swept her pale features, instantly recognising the problem, and pulled her into his arms. 'You should have told me you were afraid of heights. We're going back down.' And he held her firmly in his protective embrace, only releasing her as they stepped back onto firm ground.

Eloise glanced back up at the towering iron structure,

and still felt slightly dizzy. She leant against one of the mighty iron supports for a moment, marvelling that she'd actually had the nerve to go to the top. 'I did it.' She flashed Marcus a shaky smile.

'Yes.' He smiled back. 'But I think Les Invalides, and Napoleon's tomb next; it is underground and safe for you. Unless you are afraid of going underground as well,' he queried seriously.

She was elated that at last she had finally seen the view from the top of the world-famous tower. She had never dared do it by herself, even though she had been to Paris quite a few times in the past months—and, surprised by Marcus's apparent concern, her luscious lips parted in a beaming grin. 'Marcus, you're fussing like an old woman,' she giggled.

An arrested expression flickered across his handsome face, and he closed the space between them. He braced his hands on the iron beam either side of her, and covered her mouth with his. And there at the foot of the Eiffel Tower, in broad daylight, with hundreds of people watching, he kissed her with a hunger, a fiery brand of ownership that sent a wave of scorching heat racing through her veins.

'Marcus.' She gasped his name as he released her swollen lips. 'People are looking.'

'So? You're my woman,' he declared on a ragged breath. 'But you're right, I am not usually in the habit of kissing in public. But you drive me crazy.' He looked around distractedly, 'Let's go.'

Marcus could have been one of Napoleon's generals Eloise thought with secret amusement, as he proceeded to lead her to Les Invalides, then across the river to the Arc de Triomphe, and the tomb of the unknown soldier. He pointed out the matching arch over a mile away, marvelling at the skill of the architect.

They sat at a pavement café of the Champs Elysée, and

there with the local Parisians, and the obvious tourists from all over the world, they shared a bottle of wine, and a meal of light fluffy omelettes with salad. Whether it was the wine or the company, Eloise realised she really was enjoying herself. Marcus was a good conversationalist and very knowledgeable about Paris, and as if by common consent they avoided talking about anything personal. Relaxed, Eloise drained her glass and replaced it on the table. She glanced across at Marcus; he was withdrawing some money from his wallet.

'Are we leaving already?' she demanded. 'I quite like watching the world go by.'

And he loved watching her, Marcus realised, but didn't say it. 'Yes,' he confirmed. The jade silk shirt was sleeveless, and the top button was unfastened, revealing a shadowy cleavage. Intellectually, he knew she was a liar and a cheat, but it didn't stop his body responding in a most inconvenient manner.

'I plan we visit the Louvre next for approximately two hours, and then visit the Pompidou centre,' he ground out, shoving one hand in his pocket and rising to his feet.

'Very organised,' Eloise teased him but took the hand he held out to her, and let him lead her down towards the Louvre.

The queue to enter was huge...

Eloise turned laughing eyes up to Marcus, and saw the frustration in the set of his hard features. 'Finally defeated, *mon generale*,' she mocked. 'You have to wait like everyone else.'

'No, I think I have waited long enough.' He tightened his grip on her hand and surveyed her with blatant male intensity.

Suddenly tension simmered in the air between them. The crowd around them vanished and Eloise was drowning in the darkening depths of his deep brown eyes. His thumb stroked the palm of her hand and then he tugged her very gently against the hard heat of his body.

'Why wait to see an ancient work of art, when I have a perfect work of art in my grasp?' he said with blunt urgency. 'My apartment is not far.'

She wanted to lash out at him for looking at her with such arrogant possession. Yesterday she might have done but, after last night, all she could think of was his sensual mouth on hers, his large, strong, naked body possessing her.

He pulled her along the road and into the shadowed entrance hall of a large building. She could feel her heart hammering in her chest, and she could sense the powerful sexual tension that gripped his great frame. At the foot of the stairs, he glanced down at her and, as if compelled, he backed her against the wall and covered her mouth with his own in a ravishing kiss that left her boneless when he finally lifted his dark head.

'Hell! Why did I choose the top floor?' he grated and dragged her up the stairs, finally turning around and sweeping her up in his arms, for the final two flights.

He opened the door, and she was back where she had been last night. This time, Marcus didn't hesitate but marched straight into the bedroom.

Eloise didn't have time to survey her surroundings as he lowered her down the lean length of his superbly fit body. She could feel the tension in his every muscle, the faint musky scent all male and all Marcus, and she quivered, inside heat surging in her lower body.

His hands dispensed with the buttons down the front of her blouse with a speed that smacked of vast experience, but Eloise didn't care; she grasped his lean waist and hung on as he slipped her blouse from her shoulder and flicked her bra open and off.

With a groan Marcus dropped his head and suckled at

an erect dusky nipple, and her hands clenched fiercely in his waist, an involuntary groan of pleasure torn from her throat. Her head fell back, and then her whole body as Marcus eased her down on the bed and, with hands that shook slightly, divested her of her trousers and briefs.

His own clothes were shrugged off in a second and he was over her, large, lean and magnificently aroused. She was awed by his spectacular male beauty and helpless in his grasp as his strong hands swept the whole length of her slender frame. One hand swept upwards over the curve of her thigh, and with his other he caught her throat, and his mouth crashed down on her already parted lips.

His long fingers explored the silken red curls at the juncture of her thighs with devastating effect, even as his mouth trailed down her throat and back to her aching breasts. He lingered there, teasing her sensitive flesh until every nerve in her body tautened to breaking point, in fiery anticipation.

'I have to have you now,' Marcus muttered thickly.

He bit down on a distended nipple, then soothed with his tongue and she writhed beneath him, consumed by a hunger, a need so intense she cried out his name.

The sound of his name from her lush lips drove him to the edge and Marcus arched back and, cupping her bottom, he thrust deep into her hot, tight, silken sheath.

Eloise dug her fingers into the night-black hair of his head, and gave herself up in wild, wanton delight to the primitive joining. She was inflamed to fever pitch, and when he took her mouth again in a savage admission of need she returned the kiss, her tongue duelling with his. His great body stilled, fighting to retain control.

Eloise slid her hand down the indent of his spine, felt him shudder, and clenched his buttocks, needing him to move, to ease the intolerable tension, but he stayed fast.

Lifting his dark head, black eyes burning down into

hers. 'You make me…' but whatever he had been going
to say was lost as Eloise involuntarily clenched and tightened her legs around him.

He moved hard and fast and Eloise naturally, wantonly
picked up the furious rhythm and was spun into a world
of pure sensation that exploded in a shattering conflagra-
tion like a star going nova. She clung to him, whimpering
cries escaping from her.

Marcus, his breathing audible, stared down into her
dazed green eyes, and slowly eased from her allowing her
limp body to sink back on the bed. His dilated black eyes
still fixed to her, he rolled off her and, brushing her lips
with his, he leant on one elbow and stared down at her in
silence for a long moment, his large hand stroking down
her still-quivering body with a tactile delight.

'Exquisite,' Marcus murmured softly. 'I have never seen
you totally naked in the light of day,' and he dropped
another kiss on her brow.

Only then did Eloise realise it couldn't be more than
three in the afternoon, the summer sun was shinning
though the window, lighting every corner of the bedroom,
and she was stark naked with a man who was her enemy.
'Oh.' Instinctively, she crossed her arms over her breasts.

Marcus's narrowed gaze swept her hectically flushed
face, and lower to her defensive arms over her chest, and
then he burst out laughing.

'What's the joke?' she demanded, and with a speaking
glance Marcus led his gaze linger on her folded arms, and
lower to where his long leg lay over her lower body, then
back to her face.

'A bit late to be bashful, darling.' Marcus fought to re-
strain his laughter. 'After what we've just done.'

Eloise saw the humour in her defensive action, and
chuckled. 'Yes, well, I am shy.'

'You can certainly act shy,' Marcus drawled and, lifting

a finger, he traced the smiling curve of her mouth. 'But, thankfully—' he surveyed her with delighted masculine satisfaction '—in bed you are the most wonderfully passionate, sexy woman. I can't get enough of you.'

Eloise almost laughed again, but it was with sick humour. If only he knew since the age of twenty she had never looked at a man. Before that, Marcus himself had been the only male she had allowed to touch her and he still was....

Marcus scanned her naked body spread out before him, and let his finger trail from her mouth to circle the areolae of her breasts; he felt her tremor and, lifting his dark head, he scrutinised her with a reawakening of desire. A tiny muscle pulsed at the corner of his mouth. 'I doubt I will ever have enough of you,' he breathed.

Held by his darkening eyes, she was shaken by his unconcealed passion, and tore her gaze away to look somewhere over his shoulder. To believe him would be the road to hell, she knew. She could not let her guard down, but as he once more took her mouth in a hot hungry surge of passion Eloise caved in. Her hands gripped his smooth shoulders, and skimmed over the tautness of the muscles flexing in his back and, closing her eyes, she bowed to the inevitable.

'You are so hot, so tight,' Marcus rasped as once more he drove her to the heights and, groaning her name, he thrust deeply into her one last time, felt her come and then jerked violently with the force of his own release.

CHAPTER EIGHT

MARCUS flopped over onto his back carrying her with him, folding her in his arms so tenderly, for a second Eloise felt as she had the very first time they made love. But not quite... Then she had felt as though they were one single identity bound by love. Now she knew better...

Her mouth pressed a brief caress against his bronzed chest, breathing in the hot, moist scent of him. Then she lifted her head and collided with slumberous dark eyes. 'I need the bathroom,' she said prosaically and wriggled from his hold.

Standing in the shower cubicle, the warm spray beating down on her, Eloise tried to come to terms with what she had done, but before she could get her chaotic emotions in any kind of order, the door of the shower stall opened and Marcus appeared. Very tall and broad but without an inch of fat on his muscular frame, his black hair and eyes gleaming, he was magnificently male and incredibly gorgeous.

'Allow me,' he chuckled, knowing exactly what she was thinking, and took the soap from her numb fingers.

What followed was a lesson in sensuality that left Eloise weak as a kitten, and clinging limply to his wide shoulders as he carried her to the bed and tucked her in.

She groaned and rolled over on the wide bed, fighting the demons in her mind, and suddenly opened her eyes. It was dark, and for a moment she did not know where she was; then she remembered. She glanced across the bed. She was alone.

Five minutes later, dressed and with her hair combed back in a ponytail, she nervously made her way into the sitting room. Marcus was at the desk, a laptop computer open in front of him, obviously working.

What did one say after spending all afternoon in bed with a man? she thought despairingly. 'I think I'd better be going now,' was the best she could come up with.

Marcus spun around in his seat. 'Eloise, you're awake,' and, getting to his feet, in two lithe strides he was beside her. 'And you're not going anywhere. I've cancelled your hotel room.' With a wave of his hand, he indicated a suit-case on the floor. 'And arranged for your clothes to be sent here. It makes more sense to stay here while we are in Paris.' As he bent his head she knew he was going to kiss her.

Evading his mouth, she stiffened angrily. 'You…you have…my hotel room.' She could not get the words out, she was so mad at his high-handedness. 'How dare you?' she finally snapped. 'You had no right.'

Marcus stilled and studied her beneath hooded dark eyes. 'I have every right, Eloise. You gave me the right yesterday when you accepted my terms to keep you out of court.'

Reminded with such brutal candour of their deal, Eloise paled. 'I see.' And she did—he held all the cards and he was the sort of man that always won. 'But what will I tell Katy?' she murmured under her breath, but he heard her.

'I'll take care of Katy and Harry,' he said arrogantly.

With the same speed and cunning as he had taken over her life, no doubt. Pride alone made her square her shoulders and face him. 'I suppose it will be more convenient for the brief time I am in Paris,' she agreed, and, with a burning desire to hit back at him, she added with mock sweetness, 'after all, why should I spend my money on a hotel bill when I am a wealthy man's mistress? In fact I could do with some new clothes. I didn't bring much with me, because I thought I was only staying a couple of nights.'

Marcus had the gall to laugh. 'That's what I like about you, Eloise. Even when you're down you're never out.'

'Pig,' she snapped. 'I'm going to unpack.' She brushed past him to get to her suitcase.

But later that evening, once more in the wide bed, with Marcus, pig was not the word that sprang to mind. Eloise had to clench her teeth to hold back the words of love that hovered on her tongue, and repeat over and over in her head *no emotional involvement*.

When she finally had the breath to speak and her emotions under control she asked casually, 'How long have you had this place?'

A husky chuckle greeted her enquiry, and held firm against the side of his mighty body, she glanced sideways up at him. 'What's so funny?'

'You, Eloise. Together, we have just experienced mind-blowing sex.' Amused dark eyes rested quizzically on her lovely face. 'And you come out with a mundane question like that.'

Her lips compressed. 'Sorry. I didn't realise conversation was forbidden between bouts of sex.'

'Bouts of sex.' Marcus's expressive mouth curved into a sardonic smile. 'Crude, Eloise.'

'But then you are?' she snapped back.

She felt his body tense, and his fingers bit tightly into her side, and she saw the swift flare of anger in his deep brown eyes. Then the corners of his sensuous mouth quirked in a cynical smile.

'If you really think that, Eloise, then your sex education has not been as extensive as I thought. Perhaps I should show you the difference.' And, flipping her onto her back he hovered over her. Catching her hands in one of his, he pinned them above her head and kissed her.

She felt the latent passion in his kiss, but he went on kissing her, and pinned to the bed she was unable to resist. With hand and mouth he tormented her until she was drowning in something so incredibly erotic that she groaned out loud, and she was incapable of offering any protest as he roughly positioned himself between her thighs.

Her body cried out for him, and in that moment it hit her like a bolt of lightning. She loved him, always had and probably always would. It didn't matter that he was ruthless and arrogant and felt nothing for her but lust. She knew he was the only man she would ever allow to touch her, and a single emotional tear squeezed from her eye.

Marcus looked down at her and stilled. Hell what was he doing? He knew he could have her, here and now, the act primitive and yet satisfying, and it took all his will power to pull back, his body rock-hard and aching.

Eloise glanced up, her green eyes slowly focusing on Marcus, and wondered why he had stopped.

'What we share is not crude, Eloise.' He smiled a ruefully slightly humorous grin, accurately reading her mind. 'And I intend to keep it that way.'

Marcus watched the fleeting emotions of surprise, regret and finally relief chase across her exquisite features, and accurately read every one of them, amazed at his own restraint and slightly worried. He had never felt protective of his usual lady friends but for some inexplicable reason with Eloise it was different.

He paused and cleared his throat. 'Now, what was it you wanted to know? How long have I had this place?' Rolling over on his back and curving her unresisting body in the crook of his arm, he proceeded to tell her.

'My father bought this apartment for me when I spent a year here studying French. My father was of the old-fashioned school, who thought if one wanted to be a player in the world-wide business market, then it was essential to speak the two languages of diplomacy, English and French.'

Realising she loved him made her feel incredibly vulnerable but, somehow comforted by the warmth of his body and the deep melodious tone of his voice, she slowly relaxed. 'Ah, so that's why you are so fluent in French,' she murmured. 'And the London hotel—don't tell me he bought that for you as well?' Such conspicuous wealth was unimaginable to Eloise.

Marcus chuckled. 'No, I bought the hotel myself a few years later. When I was a student in London I stayed in a hall of residence. It was single-sex and very correct.'

She looked up beneath the thick fringe of her lashes. The sensual curve of his mouth brought vividly to mind how it felt on her own, and her stomach flipped. She didn't want to like him, didn't want to admit she loved him, and certainly did not want Marcus to discover how she felt, and she hid the disturbing thought with humour.

'Why is it I have difficulty associating you with correct and sex?' she posed. 'Unless, of course, you're a secret S and M freak?' she concluded with a grin.

A husky chuckle greeted her comment. 'Wishful thinking, darling.' And, leaning over her, he added, 'S and M is not my thing, but I will be perfectly happy to oblige if your fantasy is to be bound to my bed.'

'No, certainly not,' Eloise shot back, horrified at where her attempt at humour had led.

'Pity,' Marcus observed with a grin, his dark eyes laughing down at her, and wondered if she was aware she had the most expressive eyes; every flicker of emotion was recorded in the swirling emerald depths. 'Still, I think I can survive on straight sex, as long as it is with you.'

'Straight sex, with a crooked lady friend.' She said the first thing that came into her head, and then wished she hadn't as she saw the swift flare of anger in the depths of the black eyes that held hers. Then a muscle in his jaw twitched, a slow smile tilted the corners of his lips again, and he lifted a finger to trace the contours of her slightly parted lips.

'Forget the crooked part, and be my lady, and I will do the same,' Marcus offered lazily. 'The deal we made need not affect our relationship, unless we let it.' He shrugged a smooth, tanned shoulder. 'A truce, if you like.'

Pretend the deal never existed. It would be very foolish, Eloise told herself, but with Marcus's hand slipping from her lips to her throat and lower, she felt like taking the chance. His words had given her the first crumb of hope for the future. 'All right,' she agreed rather breathlessly.

'That design looks really promising.' Katy stood behind Eloise surveying the drawing board over her shoulder. 'Inspired, in fact. It just goes to show what the love of a good man can do,' Katy teased happily.

Eloise grimaced! If only that were true, she thought longingly. But Marcus's intentions were far less honourable. A lustful revenge was more what he had in mind.

'And where is he?' Katy demanded as Eloise turned in her seat to look at her friend. 'We haven't seen him for nearly a week.'

'Marcus *does* work,' Eloise drawled mockingly. 'He has an office on Wall Street, and he keeps apartments in London and Paris, but his home base is in Greece. And

hopefully, if we all work a bit harder, we might end up
with three or four outlets as well.' She diverted Katy from
any more personal questions by asking how the latest designs were selling.

It was over a month since she had returned from Paris.
The week in Paris had been a revelation to Eloise, and she
blushed at the thought. She'd spent most of it in Marcus's
wide bed. They'd eaten out occasionally, and he'd insisted
on taking her shopping and spending a fortune on clothes
for her. She'd tried to stop him, pointing out she had only
been joking when she suggested he buy her clothes, and
in any case she was only going to be with him for one
year.

His short reply was to remind her of their truce.

On returning to London, he'd insisted on accompanying
her to her apartment. She hadn't wanted him in her own
home, and she certainly hadn't wanted him to make love
to her there, but he did. She couldn't sleep in her own bed
at night without thinking of him sharing it with her.

The next evening he had called, supposedly to take her
out to dinner; instead, she had landed up in the king-sized
bed in his London penthouse, and dinner was a cheese
sandwich before, at her insistence, she returned to her own
home.

In the ensuing weeks, he had behaved as far as Katy
and Harry were concerned as the perfect suitor for their
friend, handsome, sexy but more than that—he was caring
and concerned, and his input in the business had been in-
valuable. He had a wonderful sense of humour. Eloise had
watched him joking and laughing with Jeff and Julian, and
Katy and Harry; they had all dined frequently together,
and according to all of them Marcus was wonderful.

He was the same with everyone; even baby Benjamin
gurgled when Marcus appeared. Eloise kept reminding her-

self, he was a master manipulator and a devious swine—
but, God help her, even as she hated him for what he was
doing to her, she was finding it harder and harder to retain
a semblance of distance from the man. Every night that
she spent in his bed, when he made love to her with a
passion, tenderness, or simply a ravishing hunger, it became more difficult to hold back the words of love she
ached to say.

True to his word, their affair was high profile. He'd
insisted on taking her to the premiere of a film, where
they'd been photographed, and appeared in the gossip column of a national daily the following day. Eloise cringed
at the publicity, and lived in fear of anyone making the
connection with her past. She had tried to argue with
Marcus and, to give him his due, after that one event, he'd
bowed to her wishes, and intimate restaurants, and an occasional trip to the cinema had followed.

Surprisingly, as the weeks passed, Eloise found herself
actually thinking of Marcus as a normal boyfriend. He did
nothing to dispel the notion and remarkably the truce
they'd struck in Paris was holding up. Neither ever mentioned the real reason for their togetherness. They talked,
they laughed, they made love, and the few times he
couldn't see her, he sent her flowers, and phoned every
day.

'Daydreaming won't get the work done.' Katy's voice
cut into her troubled thoughts. 'Mind you, I don't blame
you. Much as I love Harry, I can see what a wonderful
catch Marcus is. If you play your cards right, you could
keep him—wedding bells, the lot, I'm sure.'

Eloise gave a sharp laugh. 'No, I don't think so.' But
in her heart of hearts she wished it were true. It was becoming harder and harder to maintain the invisible barrier
she had erected in her mind that kept her from declaring

her love to Marcus. And lying to Katy didn't help. She longed to confide the truth to her friend, but she could imagine Katy's angry reaction if she did. *Marcus is not my boyfriend, he simply blackmailed me into being his mistress for a year and in return he won't wreck our business.* Katy would probably kill him…

'And, to answer your first question, he's in New York and likely to stay there for a while. And, knowing Marcus, I doubt if he'll be missing me for long. There are too many beautiful women in the world ready to accommodate him.'

'Your trouble is, you don't realise how lovely you are, both inside and out. But Marcus knows, I'm sure.'

'Thanks for the compliment, Katy, and I hope you're right.' Eloise forced a grin and, turning back to her drawing board, she added, 'But in the meantime I suggest you and I get back to work,' and resumed sketching.

Freedom was a funny thing Eloise mused, as she strolled down Kensington High Street on the second Friday of Marcus's absence. Retail therapy, Katy had said as she'd told Eloise to take off for the afternoon.

Eloise had told herself she was glad to be on her own again, free to spend her time as she chose, but the reality was she missed Marcus's lovemaking—even if it was just sex—and yes, she missed his company. She missed him…

Marcus had stipulated one year as his mistress, and to her horror last night she had actually caught herself working out how many weeks she had left, and resenting his time away from her. He was stunningly attractive, and she had heard New York was full of bright, beautiful women. Alone with her thoughts, she was eaten up with jealousy and finally realised Marcus might not even stay a year with her…

She knew he wasn't actually bothered about the money

she was supposed to be paying in kind. How could he be, when he spent a fortune on clothes and presents for her? She comforted herself with the thought perhaps he had got over his original anger, and genuinely enjoyed her company.

More and more over the past weeks Eloise had the growing conviction Marcus was truly beginning to care for her on a deeper level. He showed it in so many ways— flowers, an exquisite antique emerald and diamond necklace with matching earrings. She'd tried to refuse, but he wouldn't let her, telling her it was a memento of their time in Paris, and had actually belonged to some duchess who was beheaded in the French revolution.

Sometimes the present was small, a single rose, and sometimes ridiculous, like when he left for New York and he presented her with a tiny ugly troll, and demanded, 'Promise me this is the only male you will look at while I am away.' Giggling, she'd promised and they'd made wonderful love. He telephoned her first thing in the morning British time, from his bed as it was about two in the morning in New York, and he liked to talk to her before going to sleep. She found it endearing, and it fed the hope that was growing in her heart that her love for him had a chance.

He was coming back next Tuesday and her spirit lifted at the thought, and she walked into Harrods with a smile on her face. A negligée to knock Marcus's eyes out, she decided. Stopping by the perfume counter, she picked up a tester, and was about to spray some ruinously expensive scent on her wrist when a familiar voice called her name.

'Eloise. How are you?'

She dropped the bottle back on the counter and turned around.

'Ted. Ted Charlton, I have a bone to pick with you,'

she said bluntly, but she could not help smiling at his sheepish expression.

'Guilty,' he held up his hand. 'I know what you're going to say, but let me take you out for an early dinner, and I'll explain.'

It was a warm summer evening and a long, lonely week-end stretched before her. She had nothing planned for to-night other than returning home and watching television. Why not? she thought.

'Yes, okay.' She waited while he bought a bottle of perfume.

'I have a hot date Saturday night,' he explained with a chuckle. 'Let's find somewhere to get a drink and then we'll eat, and I'll confess all my sins.'

Ted found them a great French restaurant and ordered a couple of Martinis, a bottle of good wine and the food.

'I saw the pictures of you and Marcus in the press, and I can guess why you want to talk to me.' Ted's comment came over the aperitif.

Eloise took a moment to find her voice. 'Marcus appears to be under the impression you and I...' She cleared her throat, suddenly embarrassed.

'I know what you're trying to say.' Ted helped her out. 'And I'm sorry, I shouldn't have lied. But try and under-stand from my point of view, Eloise.'

'I'm listening,' she said quietly.

'Marcus Kouvaris is a lot younger than me—very hand-some, very successful, very clever.' Ted lifted his glass and drained it, looking rather wry.

One delicate brow arched quizzically. 'So?' she prompted.

'Well, it doesn't show me in a very favourable light.'

'Ted, forget the light—just tell me what happened,' Eloise said bluntly.

'It was really my ex-wife's fault. Her lawyer did me for

millions, and I had a very sweet deal, almost completed. No disrespect to KHE, but it was worth a lot more than your small business, I was short of cash, and I needed the money quick. I knew Marcus Kouvaris was in town, and I remembered the way he'd looked at you.'

'The way he looked at me? What on earth has that to do with your business dealings?' she asked, totally confused.

'I'm a man; I know how the male psyche works. So I approached Kouvaris to take my share of KHE off my hands. I knew he could easily afford it, and it would earn him Brownie points with you. I wasn't wrong; he agreed immediately.'

'You mean, you think Marcus bought in to KHE to please me?' The enormity of what Ted was suggesting boggled her mind, until she remembered the blackmail. But, even so, Ted's suggestion made her think... Marcus had not gone deliberately seeking shares in KHE, so that must mean something.

'Of course, Eloise, you are a stunningly beautiful woman and a talented artist as well. There isn't a man alive who wouldn't fancy you, believe me.'

'Flattery, Ted, won't get you off the hook. I want to know why you lied to Marcus about you and me.'

'You can put it down to an old man's pride or sour grapes. I invited Marcus to have dinner at my hotel to celebrate the deal, and then at my insistence we retired to the bar. What can I say?' He shrugged his broad shoulders. 'I had too much to drink and this exquisite blonde I had been trying to impress for the past few days made it very obvious she wasn't interested in me—but that she fancied Marcus instead. He made it obvious he wasn't interested, and when she finally gave up and left, after giving me the cold shoulder, I was feeling pretty miserable. So when

Marcus asked exactly how well I knew you—' He hesitated, his face turning a dull shade of red.

At least he had the grace to blush, Eloise thought, holding Ted's blue eyes with her own. 'Go on.'

'I lied and said we'd spent the night together. It was male ego, and plain old-fashioned jealousy. First my ex-wife rejected me, and then the girl in the hotel who'd been quite happy to drink with me the night before only had eyes for Kouvaris. There's only so much rejection one man can take. I admit I was drunk and I didn't see why Marcus should get away worry-free, and if my stupid lie has hurt you in any way I'm sorry.'

Eloise shook her head. 'It doesn't matter, Ted.' The fact Marcus had turned down the other woman made her feel generous. 'I forgive you.'

'You love the guy.'

'Something like that,' she said with a smile. Marcus was not quite the devil she tried to paint him, she knew, and a tiny seed of hope rooted in her brain. Maybe her love for Marcus was not completely futile…

The food arrived and was excellent. It was nice to sit and chat with the ease of old friends; Ted was one of the few men she was comfortable with. Later, when Ted got her a cab to go home and insisted on accompanying her, she made no objection. She even asked him in for coffee…

Marcus swung out of the taxi, and leapt up the few steps to the entrance door of the Georgian building. He lifted a finger to press the bell for Eloise's apartment and realised the door was open. Careless, but it suited his purpose. He wanted to surprise Eloise, and the tingling sense of anticipation at the thought of seeing her again lent speed to his long legs, as he ran up the two flights of stairs without catching his breath.

He'd spoken to her on the telephone late last night and

told her he wouldn't be back until next week. But after putting the phone down, having heard the husky sound of her voice ringing in his ears, he'd wanted her so badly he'd cancelled some meetings and crammed the rest into a couple of hours in the morning, and taken the next flight out of New York.

Marcus moved towards the door at the end of the hallway. He could hear the sound of voices. Good: she was home, and obviously watching the television. His hand grasped the door handle; it yielded to the pressure and he strode across the tiny inner hall, and into the sitting room.

'Eloise, darling.' She spun around in surprise at the entrance to the hall that led to the bedroom, and the breath caught in his throat.

Marcus's gaze flew over her. Her red hair framed a startled but incredibly beautiful face and fell in a tumbling mass of curls over her creamy shoulders. Her body was encased in a wisp of blue silk, tiny straps supporting the slip-styled dress that ended a few inches above her knees. There was no mistaking the firm thrust of her breasts or the tightening of her nipples as she stared at him, and what held him transfixed was not the shock that widened her brilliant emerald eyes, but the sheer wonder of her smile that followed.

'Marcus, you're back!' Eloise cried in delight. 'I wasn't expecting you until next week.' She blinked; it really was Marcus, looking staggeringly handsome in a perfectly tailored silver-grey business suit. But it was the glittering warmth in his dark eyes, especially for her, that made her breath catch.

He started slowly towards her. 'I cancelled the rest of my business meetings,' he declared throatily. 'I wanted to surprise you.'

CHAPTER NINE

IT TOOK every bit of will power she possessed to stop herself running to him and throwing her arms around him. 'Marcus.' She licked her lips nervously. 'I'm...' *Glad to see you*, was what she had been going to say. What a cop-out! He was her lover, and she loved him, and courageously she decided to try honesty. 'I've missed you.' After all, he had returned early; that had to mean something.

He stopped when he was inches away from her. 'Eloise,' he husked. His dark eyes, blazing with desire, scanned her and, reaching out, he folded her in his arms and covered her mouth with his own.

His mouth was hot and searching with a hungry intensity that she met and matched. Eloise whispered his name as his tongue parted her lips. She arched against him and wound her arms around his neck, her hands stroking the silken hair at the nape, before sweeping lovingly across his powerful shoulders.

'So long,' Marcus groaned and pressed her body to his. 'Too long.' He could feel the rounded fullness of her breasts crushed against his chest. This was what he had come back for...

She was all woman; the scent of her, the soft curves and long shapely legs, promised and beguiled. He moulded her buttocks and lifted her, the seductive tilt of her pelvis fitting into the cradle of his hips, as he ground his rock-hard length against her in raw need.

'Ooops, sorry.'

Marcus jerked his head back, his black gaze clashing with the blue of Ted Charlton. The man had obviously just strolled into the room from the direction of the bedroom. Marcus felt the breath leave his body as though he had been punched in the gut, and for a second a red haze of rage blinded him. He swore violently in Greek, and abruptly thrust Eloise away from him. 'You bitch.'

Eloise stumbled back, her eyes widening in horror as she realised what it must look like. 'No. It's not like…' She looked up at Marcus and ground to a halt. The change in him was devastating. Incredulous rage clenched his hard dark features, a muscle jerking uncontrollably in his taut cheek.

'Then what is he doing here?' Marcus's eyes burnt into hers. 'Or shall I guess?' he drawled with cynical contempt. 'A week without sex and you're anyone's.' His gaze sliced back to Ted, apparently unable to believe what he was seeing.

Eloise was shaking, terrified by the cold deadly look in Marcus's eyes; but beneath the terror she had a hysterical desire to laugh at his contemptuous conclusion she could not live without sex for more than a week. If only he knew…

She grabbed his arm. 'No, Marcus, listen to me. I bumped into Ted in a department store; he was shopping for perfume for his girlfriend, and I challenged him to explain what he meant by telling you I had slept with him.'

'I just bet you did. Persuaded him to lie for you?'

'Damn it, *no*.' Eloise cut him off. 'Ted lied to you; he told me the truth over dinner.' She tightened her grip on his jacket as he would have pulled away. 'All about your celebration dinner and getting drunk and the girl in the bar. He told you he slept with me because he was jealous of you. Surely you can see that…?' she prompted desperately.

'All I see is a conniving lying bitch,' he snarled, his black eyes blazing, 'who would sell her body for the price of a dinner,' and she knew he hadn't believed a word she'd said.

The Marcus she loved didn't exist, she realised with blinding clarity. He was a figment of a nineteen-year-old's imagination. She didn't recognise the man towering over her, dark and dangerous, but for Ted's sake she tried once more to defuse the situation.

'I shared dinner with Ted because he wanted to explain and apologise to me for lying about me to you, nothing more—and if you're too pig-headed to see that, tough.'

Marcus took a step towards her and he lifted her hand off his sleeve, then he stopped. Her green eyes clashed with his; she saw the fury and contempt and thought, What was the point?

All that linked her and Marcus was sex. A shameful passion on her side she was helpless to control, and a virile man's lust powered by revenge on his. Marcus did not love her, and never would, and that was the greatest pain of all. She took a deep shuddering breath and suddenly Ted was pushing Eloise to one side and facing Marcus.

'If you want to lash out at anyone, Kouvaris, try me.'

Marcus's hand shot out and he grabbed Ted by the collar and slammed him back against the wall. 'Don't tempt me,' he snarled. He wanted to smash the man's face to a pulp and he didn't question the reason.

'You're a fool, Kouvaris,' Ted grated in a high-pitched voice, nearly choking and clutching at Marcus's hands.

'I can beat the hell out of you, any day, in any way,' Marcus raged, his violence controlled by a thread.

'I know,' Ted shot back. 'That's why I lied and said I'd

slept with Eloise. I saw the way you looked at Eloise the first time I met you,' he stated cynically. 'And I saw the way the girl in the bar looked at you, when the night before she had been all over me. I was drunk, I was jealous and I lied. Rejected by a wife and a bar-girl, I was damned if I was going to make it easy for you to get Eloise. Lousy, I know, but that's the truth.'

The two men stared at each other. Ted's face red and Marcus's grey beneath his tan, only his eyes blazing black with rage.

For a long moment Eloise simply stared at the scene before, all her energy concentrated on fighting the awful pain she was trying to hide. But as she watched the pain dissolved into a quite different emotion.

They were like two stags at bay, both ruthless powerful men, leaders of the pack. She recognised the angry acknowledgement between them—the old giving way to the young, but not without a fight—and a slow-burning anger ignited in her breast.

This was her home, her life. Pride stiffened her spine. She didn't have to justify her actions to any man, certainly not the two egotistical male chauvinists before her, who were scrapping like two dogs over a bone. And in her living room!

'Right, that's it! Cut it out,' she yelled. 'And both of you can get out.'

Marcus shot her a look of outraged incredulity. She was ordering him out… He was the injured party in this debacle.

She met his gaze, her green eyes sparking fire, and she might have laughed if she hadn't been so angry, Marcus looked so put out! 'Let him go,' she snapped.

Slowly, Marcus released his iron grip on Ted's collar and some of the rage faded from his eyes. She was standing tall and proud, her luscious body bristling with tension. She was beautiful when she was angry. She was beautiful any time, and lost in passion beneath him she was paradise. Whether she and Ted were telling the truth or not, was he prepared to give up all that simmering sexuality? The tightening in his groin answered for him. Hell, no—not yet.

Marcus glanced back at Ted. 'I think it's time you left,' he grated through his teeth. 'Eloise is mine.' His narrowed eyes fixed on Ted, his great body tense and towering threateningly over his rival. 'You understand?'

'Do you?' Ted murmured dryly, shaking his head. He walked past Marcus. And, for sheer devilment, stopped and dropped a light kiss on Eloise's cheek. 'So long and good luck, and if you ever need me get in touch.'

'You're pushing your luck,' Marcus growled, taking a step towards him.

'No.' Ted grinned back and, picking up the gift-wrapped bottle of perfume from the table where he had placed it earlier, he waved it in front of Marcus's face. 'I never trust to luck. I have a hot date tomorrow night, and I know how to treat a lady, unlike some.' Laughing, he strolled out of the apartment.

Her legs trembling, Eloise sat down on the nearest sofa. 'I think you'd better leave.' Marcus had claimed her as his, as though she was an inanimate object, instead of an intelligent woman with thoughts and feelings. Well, he could go to hell, for all she cared. She had had enough.

'No,' Marcus bit out, crossing the space between them in one lithe stride. 'I cancelled my plans for the next few days to see you, and I haven't changed my mind.'

He looked down at Eloise. Maybe she was innocent where Ted was concerned. Ted had been very drunk in New York, and bitching at losing his wife and a ton of money. He vaguely remembered Ted introducing him to the blonde bimbo, and then she had been all over Marcus like a rash, so much so he had been quite rude to get rid of her.

As for the rest—his dark eyes roamed over Eloise. She was watching him, her green eyes cool, her luscious mouth held in a grim line. The red-gold tumble of her hair falling over her silky-smooth shoulders, so proud, so brave, and he was yelling at her like a loony.

If he was honest, he doubted she'd ever been involved with her mother's scam. He'd seen the company books, and discovered the company had been set up nine months after Chloe's death. Harry had told him the initial finance was from Eloise's inheritance from her late mother's estate. Eloise had bought the premises. Realistically, Eloise should be the major shareholder, and yet according to the records they were three equal partners, all drawing the same salary. If Eloise was a gold-digger, as he had thought, then she had a very funny way of going about it. Katy and Harry would not have a business if it were not for Eloise.

She was probably innocent of all he had accused her of, and incredibly generous to those she considered friends. Marcus suddenly realised he wanted to be in that company, to bask in Eloise's approval. He'd known a lot of women in his life, some almost as beautiful and with the same luscious curves as Eloise—well, no, not quite as perfect, but some a lot more sexually aggressive in bed. But he also knew with absolute certainty none had come close to affecting him the way she did.

If he'd ever caught any other woman he was involved with alone with another man, he would have walked out the door and out of the woman's life without a second thought. It scared the hell out of him that he couldn't do that with Eloise.

Since the day he'd first met her as a young girl, she'd never really left his mind and, after the last weeks together, the happiest in all his thirty-four years, she had become an obsession. An obsession that had made him act out of character, and dash back early from the USA, his business incomplete, simply to see her. She was a fever in his blood, and he intended to keep her until the fever burnt out. A secret obsession Eloise need never be aware of, but he would have to watch her more carefully in the future. Innocent or not, there would be no more Teds... He would take her home tomorrow, he concluded arrogantly.

Marcus was still here and he still wanted her. Eloise did not know whether to laugh or cry. She could hear her heart thudding in shock, an erratic rhythm against her breast-bone. Marcus must be able to hear it in the tense silence, but she dared not look at him; instead, she asked the one vital question.

'So, now do you believe I never had an affair with Ted?' Her eyes focused on the floor. It suddenly seemed imperative to her that Marcus showed some tiny bit of faith in her.

'It's not important. Forget it; I have.'

Her head came back at that, her eyes fixing on his in bitter resentment. She loved him but right at this moment she hated him. He didn't trust her an inch and never would, but still she decided to give him one last chance. The final test, she told herself.

'You saw the perfume Ted had bought. I told you we met by accident,' she said through tight lips. 'I told you Ted had lied and he confirmed it.'

One ebony brow arched in sardonic amusement. 'So you did,' he mused as he sank down on the sofa beside her. He was too close and her pulse leapt at his nearness.

'Will anything convince you?' she asked flatly. 'Spelling it out in blood, maybe?'

Marcus ran a comprehensive eye over her and, reaching out, he let his long fingers tangle in her silky red hair. 'If you want to convince me—' his voice deepened '—feel free to try.'

She had her answer. Sex was all Marcus wanted from her. She tried to pull her head away but he wouldn't let her escape. Her stormy eyes clashed with mocking black and his long fingers in her hair tightened their grip. 'It should be fun,' he teased.

'That's all I am to you, a sex game, you egotistical bastard,' Eloise shot back, her fury edged with fear as his dark head descended. She tensed, eyes wide and glinting with defiance. She was damned if she was going to roll over again beneath his sensual onslaught. That was all she had done since they met in Paris and it had to stop, she told herself.

But her traitorous pulse raced into overdrive as Marcus covered her lips with his own in an explosive kiss. His dark head blocked out the light and his hand curved around her waist, hard and restraining, while he plundered her mouth at will.

Her pulse raced, and she gripped his arms in a last-ditch attempt to break free. But he wouldn't let her go. He simply flattened her to the sofa. His hard, hot body sprawled on top of her, and his mouth continued to ravage her own, rough and then tender as one long hand swept down her body, and back to cup her breast.

She fought for control. 'No,' she moaned against his lips, struggling to breathe, denying the sensations he was forcing her to feel. Her nipples tautened into tight buds, and she trembled, unable to control her treacherous body's reaction. But by a supreme effort of will she lashed out at him with fist and knee.

He reared back, and she caught a brief glimpse of his stunned expression as she flung herself over the arm of the sofa and landed on her feet.

'What the hell was that for?' Marcus sat back against the sofa, rubbing a hand across his cheek.

'Figure it out for yourself.' Her chest heaving, she stood a few feet away, staring down at him with angry green eyes. How it was possible one man could be so infinitely desirable, a great lover, and yet be completely lacking in the emotional department Eloise did not know.

Marcus's eyes were dark and glinting with suppressed anger, and with an impatient gesture he got to his feet and moved towards her. 'You're mad because I chased Ted.'

Eloise swallowed unevenly. 'No, not that you chased him,' she said quietly. 'But that you never believed him and, more importantly, me.'

His dark eyes pinned hers, shrewd and penetrating. 'You want me to believe you; it bothers you that I don't. Why is that, I wonder? Perhaps you care for me rather more than your sharp tongue will admit.'

Any minute his clever mind would work out how she really felt about him, and she couldn't let that happen. 'No, but I object to being treated like a whore, a woman who will sleep with a man one minute and quite happily sleep with another an hour later, and by your actions that's how you see me.'

'Ah, Eloise.' Marcus's expression was grim. He looked at her standing there, so young and looking so incredibly sexy and yet innocent at the same time, and it gave him a peculiar feeling in the region of his heart that was almost pain. 'I only ever think of you as a clever, incredibly beautiful woman, and you shame us both by thinking otherwise,' he said gently and, reaching out, he caught her shoulders and drew her gently towards him. 'And if I gave you the wrong impression, I'm sorry.' He moved one hand towards her cheek, and trailed gentle fingers down until he reached her chin.

A betraying pulse began to beat at the base of her throat and a nervous flutter stirred her stomach. 'That's a first.' She tried for sarcasm, but the tremble in her voice gave her away as he tilted her chin and looked deep into her wide emerald eyes.

His eyes grew dark. He brushed her mouth gently. 'And I do believe you about Ted.'

'You do?' She stared at him, and her heart skipped a beat. He believed her. Was she hearing right? A heady excitement bubbled through her.

'Yes, I do.' Tension snaked through Marcus's large powerful body. His hand slipped from her shoulder to tighten around her slender waist, and he smoothed a few tendrils of glorious red hair from her brow. He had to keep it light, he wasn't yet ready to confess he was blinded by jealousy.

'After all, any woman with me as her lover wouldn't look twice at Ted,' he said with a husky chuckle, his slumberous dark eyes holding hers.

Eloise couldn't help it; even when she was angry, he had the ability with a word, a look, a touch to make her change her mind. Her lips twitched. 'You arrogant devil!' She shook her head but he looked deep into her green eyes and saw the humour she couldn't quite hide.

'But you like me,' he murmured teasingly, and suddenly Marcus, who had never considered if a woman liked him or not, found he was waiting, his heart pounding for her answer.

'Yes, you could say that,' she responded with a husky

chuckle of her own, and then very gently, almost reverently, he bent his head and kissed her, and she kissed him back in helpless surrender.

He gently pulled her dress off her shoulders, his dark gaze flicking over her pouting breasts, raising her in his arms, slowly with the tip of his tongue he circled the areolae of one hard nipple.

'Oh, yes,' she sighed, immediately thrown back into a whirlpool of sensations. 'Please.'

'Oh, yes,' Marcus parroted, his mouth enclosing the rigid tip and slowly licking her aching flesh, teasing with tongue and teeth until her back arched, and she was burning with the heady heat of passion and desperate need for continuance.

He slipped his arms beneath her, lifting her high so he could capture her mouth with his in a long drugging kiss as he carried her into the bedroom. He slid her down the long length of his body, letting her feel the pulsing ache of his arousal as he eased her out of her dress in one smooth movement.

He was wearing too many clothes. A low groan of frustration escaped her and she pushed her hands beneath his jacket up and around his back, dragging his head down to her, finding his mouth with her own.

Airborne again, Marcus laid her down on the bed, and in seconds joined her naked. A deep erotic sigh of pleasure escaped her, as the black hair of his chest rubbed against her turgid nipples.

Long fingers traced the length of her body, the indentation of her waist, the silky softness of her flat belly, and she trembled. She gripped his shoulders quivering with need. But he played with her mouth, licking and nibbling, then thrusting with his tongue, and all the time his long fingers slowly stroked the curve of her hip, the smooth skin of her inner thigh, but frustratingly refraining from touching her where she longed to be touched.

'Marcus,' she panted, her small hands sliding down to cover his, lost to everything but her own need.

'Tell me what you want,' Marcus rasped in a dark undertone, his breath fanning her cheek, his night-black eyes searching emerald. 'Perhaps this?'

Her whole body jerked as his seeking fingers parted the velvet folds of flesh to touch the hot, moist, pulsing point of pleasure, sending convulsive shivers lancing through her.

Her hands roamed feverishly over his shoulders and skated down his back, around his broad chest to trace the silky black line down over his taut stomach, driven by a purely female primeval need to possess and be possessed, to claim him as her own. Her slender fingers found him, curving around the satin-coated steel length of him with shivering excitement, stroking him, made bold by her need.

She felt his great body shudder, and briefly she felt an incredible sense of power. But a heartbeat later she could not think at all as his mouth caught hers in a savagely hungry kiss. Involuntarily her fingers tightened around him.

With a guttural groan, Marcus raised his head. 'You do it,' he spelt out roughly, his night-black eyes clashing with her dazed green. Shuddering on the edge in a passion-induced dream, she did...

Eloise awoke early the next morning and yawned widely. She stretched languorously and was instantly aware of the warm male body beside her. Slowly turning her head, her green eyes widened on the sleeping figure of Marcus.

He lay on his back, one arm trailing across the top of

her pillow, the other flung across the other side of the bed. The sheet was draped low across his hips, his broad hair-roughened chest rising slowly and evenly in sleep.

She glanced up at his face. With his eyes closed, and a day's growth of beard darkening his firm jaw, he looked less than his perfect self, younger and somehow vulnerable.

Heat coloured her cheeks as she recalled last night, and her own part in it. She had actually touched him intimately with hands and mouth, something she had never imagined doing, and yet with Marcus she wanted to. It was unbelievable…

He was amazing. They had made love with a passion a hunger that lasted for hours until, sated and exhausted, she had fallen into a dreamless sleep. Her love-swollen lips curved in a smile of pure female satisfaction. Hardly surprising he was still asleep, she thought, her fascinated gaze sliding over his naked torso.

Even with her body aching in muscles she never knew she had, she couldn't keep her eyes off his gorgeous bronzed body, and recalling how it felt to be thoroughly possessed by him made her shudder with remembered pleasure. Unable to resist, she reached out her hand and gently smoothed the soft black hair from the centre of his chest down to the narrow strip that disappeared beneath the sheet.

'Hmm. That's nice,' Marcus murmured, moving and pressing a kiss on the top of her head.

'I thought you were asleep.' Eloise blushed scarlet and lay back, feeling almost happy. Marcus had said last night he believed her about Ted. A giant step forward—surely it couldn't be long before he believed she was innocent of all he had accused her of?

'I was, until you assaulted me.' Marcus grinned and sat

up, pulling her up with him. The dark eyes that met hers danced with wicked humour, and she smiled back.

'Me?' she questioned in mock indignation.

'Yes,' Marcus answered, and after kissing her thoroughly he rolled off the bed. 'I'll make breakfast, you start packing. We're going to Greece.'

'You're kidding, of course,' she exclaimed, her eyes skimming over his lithe body and wondering how a naked man could still manage to portray such stunning arrogance.

'I couldn't possibly leave London at the moment,' she said easily, thinking of all the new designs she was involved with for their expanding business, and Katy's light workload because of her preoccupation with Benjamin. Which was only as it should be, Eloise thought, her mind wandering into the realms of fantasy, imagining what a baby with Marcus as a father would look like.

The thought brought her up cold, all the colour leaching from her face... She looked at him as he turned back to face her, and watched the humour vanish, and his face grow cool and distant.

His dark knowing eyes rested on her pale face. 'You can and you will, Eloise. You have far too many distractions in London.' He knew he sounded harsh, but he couldn't help it; she had looked at him, white-faced and horrified, and it gave him a peculiar feeling in the area of his heart again.

How could he have gone from wanting, needing and believing her to this hard-faced tyrant, Eloise wondered, within minutes of waking up? A night of passion meant nothing to Marcus, and his complete lack of emotion simply confirmed what she already knew.

But she lived here, Eloise reminded herself firmly. She worked here. He had to be crazy. She couldn't drop everything and swan off to Greece at his say-so...

'Don't be ridiculous.'

'I would be ridiculous if I left you here alone again. On Rykos, when I am not around, my family and friends will take care of you.' Marcus knew from experience how difficult it was to have a sex life on the tiny island without everyone knowing about it, and he was a man... For Eloise, branded as his woman, it would be impossible. No man would go near her, and that suited him just fine.

'I do not need taking care of,' she fumed. Where did he get off ordering her around? Well, she wasn't putting up with it any more and she was damn well going to tell him so, but before she could open her mouth again he'd left.

She listened to him running the shower in the bathroom, and expelled a shuddering sigh. What was the point of arguing with him? she decided with bitter resentment. After the night they'd spent together, she'd had high hopes Marcus might begin to trust her, might care about her. But he'd made it brutally clear he didn't. Her mind in turmoil—Greece apart—it had hit her when thinking about babies. Marcus was always meticulous about using protection, but last night he had forgotten...

Half an hour later, she joined him in the kitchen. As she walked towards him, clad in well-washed denim jeans and a baggy grey tee-shirt, she was aware she looked a mess, and didn't give a damn. She wasn't going anywhere and that was final.

'You're wearing that to travel?' he asked flatly. 'Hardly flattering, and jeans are far too hot for August in Greece.'

'I'm not going to Greece. I have neither the time nor the inclination,' she told him coldly, pulling out a chair and sitting opposite him at the tiny kitchen table, surprised he had actually prepared coffee, toast and a selection of conserves. He wasn't totally hopeless in the kitchen, she thought dryly, suddenly feeling hungry. She filled a cup with coffee, took a sip, and reached for a slice of toast, before bravely raising cool green eyes to his. 'Some other time, perhaps.'

Marcus's gaze narrowed and swept over her tensely held body perched on the chair. She was nowhere near as confident as she tried to appear. 'Nice try, Eloise,' he drawled mockingly. 'But it isn't a request, it's an order.'

'Tough. I have to work, and I have a commitment to Katy.'

'Need I remind you, we have a deal? Your first commitment is to me and, as for your work, you can design as easily in Greece as in London.'

His deliberate mention of their deal hit her like a cruel blow, and she despised herself for harbouring a lingering shred of hope that he would grow to love her. When was she going to learn? Pride alone made her squeeze back the tears that threatened and, lifting her head, she said, 'But I don't want to,' bravely defying him.

Hooded dark eyes surveyed her. 'You don't have a choice.'

'So this is the end of the truce,' she snapped back.

Marcus cast her a cynical smile. 'Yes, if that's how you want to see it. But why pretend, Eloise? We both know I only have to touch you to make you change your mind.'

Stunned at his arrogance, her appetite deserted her, and the toast dropped from her fingers. Her gaze skated helplessly over him. He was wearing the same clothes he had arrived in last night. He should have looked a mess. But the grey designer suit fitted him like a glove, the jacket straining over broad muscular shoulders; even the blue shirt still looked perfect. How did he do it? Or was it her?

God help her! But she was made humiliatingly aware that he only spoke the truth, and it shamed her to the depths of her soul. She felt so vulnerable. What was he doing to her? A vivid mental image of last night heated her flesh, the images so real, she could almost feel the touch of his hot, hard body against her skin.

The doorbell rang and she leapt to her feet, almost stumbling on her headlong flight through the small hall to open the door. He was insidiously taking over her life; she did not seem to have the strength to deny him, and it terrified her.

Katy walked in. 'Your paper.' She dropped the paper in the direction of the hall table, lifting her head and sniffing the air. 'Is that coffee I smell?' and she headed for the kitchen.

Eloise closed the door and bent down to pick the paper off the floor. It had fallen open, and her eyes caught a name in the centre page. Rick Pritchard. The blood drained from her face, her hand shook and, closing her eyes, she paused for a moment. Then with slow deliberation she rose and folded the paper and placed it on the table.

The name was a timely reminder. It was way past time she got herself back under control. She had allowed Marcus to break through the shield she kept over her emotions, the only person to do so in four years. She must rebuild her defence against him. But how easy that was going to be with Marcus calling all the shots? A deep, shuddering sigh escaped her and, straightening her shoulders, she took a few long steadying breaths, practising the exercises she had been taught. She could hear Katy's voice and the deep rich tones of Marcus's and then laughter.

If there were any repercussions from the unprotected sex of last night, Eloise knew she would have to leave Marcus. Which meant she would have to sell the house and break up the partnership. The sound of Katy's laughter would be a thing of the past, as would their friendship, and all because of Marcus Kouvaris. But at this particular point in time she did not care. She had more important things to worry about, like staying alive… Suddenly Greece seemed a very desirable location.

By the time Eloise entered the kitchen, Marcus had talked Katy into believing it was a marvellous idea for Eloise to go to Greece. Eloise put up a token argument, not wanting Marcus to realise she had changed her mind—not because of him or Katy, but because Eloise wanted to be anywhere but England…

A dark skinned maid escorted her up a palatial marble staircase and along a wide corridor, and into a bedroom. 'The master's,' she said with a giggle.

Eloise looked at the girl blankly. 'Thank you, that will be all,' she murmured, surprisingly not in the least embarrassed, and watched as the young maid backed out of the door and shut it behind her.

Her beautiful face impassive she glanced around. Large, it was sumptuously elegant with a huge bed on a raised dais as the main feature. She strolled across the mosaic floor and pushed open a door to a sybaritic bathroom, in black and gold, with a large circular spa bath, double shower, and marble and mirrored walls. It fitted the man, she thought idly, and re-entered the bedroom and crossed to the window that took the place of one wall. She slid it open and stepped out onto a long balcony. The air was hot and heavily scented after the coolness of the bedroom, and the view so spectacular she caught her breath.

A paved patio with a dolphin-shaped swimming pool as its centre led to a garden that was a riot of colour in the early evening sun, and gently sloped down to a low wall, and a sandy beach and the clear blue sea beyond. She glanced to one side and saw an orchard, a mass of orange and lemon trees, and in the distance she could see the small cluster of luxury villas. None so luxurious as this, she was sure, and *one* the scene of the drama five years ago that had led to the tragedy her life had become now, she thought bitterly. She looked in the opposite direction and her heart missed a beat. She recognised the cliff and the precarious path down to the hidden bay.

Abruptly, she turned back to the bedroom. Marcus had brought her to his home on Rykos... A house, he had told her on the flight across, he had designed and had built in the last couple of years. What he had not told her was it was in close proximity to the cliff and beach where he and Eloise had once shared a picnic.

Eloise had kept the memory of that one perfect day in her heart and head as a kind of talisman. In times of great pain and stress, she used to conjure up the bay in her mind, to blank the horror out. It was ironic that, after reading that hated name, Rick Pritchard, in the paper this morning and, rigid with shock, she needed her talisman view, and there it was before her very eyes—and it did not work any more.

The innocent nineteen-year-old had finally gone forever. Marcus had made sure of that; and, the truly sad part was, he had not even noticed...

CHAPTER TEN

METHODICALLY Eloise unpacked her clothes, placing them in the wardrobe and drawers provided in the dressing room, deliberately avoiding looking at the masses of male garments.

'What on earth are you doing?'

On her knees, placing the last of her underclothes in a scented drawer, Eloise glanced up. Marcus was towering in the doorway, barefoot, and obviously paused in the process of undressing. The trousers of his suit were unfastened and hanging perilously on his lean hips. His shirt was open to the waist, revealing a hard, muscular chest shaded with black hair. He was a powerful, virile male, she thought almost objectively. Then she saw the expression on his darkly handsome face, one of arrogant astonishment.

He expected to be waited on hand and foot. He had probably dropped his shoes, jacket and tie in a trail across the bedroom floor, she guessed. 'What's it look like? I'm unpacking,' she said facetiously. 'It's what we lesser mortals do.'

Hooded black eyes narrowed on hers. 'I employ staff for such things.'

'Yes, O lord and master,' she muttered under her breath.

'I heard that,' Marcus drawled silkily. 'And as long as you remember it, we'll get along fine.'

He scanned her wide green eyes, anticipating her angry rebuttal, but surprisingly she simply said, 'Okay,' and stood up.

'Wait.' He caught her arm as she would have walked

past him, inexplicably angered by her apparent indifference. 'The staff are employed to take care of my guests; they are happy to have a job, and will be insulted if you do not use them.' He sounded like a pompous prig, he knew, and the knowledge made him frown in self-disgust.

Eloise glanced at the hand on her bare arm, and up into his thunderously frowning face. 'Yes... okay.'

Damn it. She was doing it again, with the *okay*, and he didn't like it one bit. Thinking about it now, he realised she had been doing it ever since Katy had lent her voice to his, in persuading Eloise to agree to come to Greece with him. She had been the same on the plane.

His dark eyes narrowed intently on her lovely face for a long moment. But her usual brilliant green eyes returned his scrutiny expressionlessly; something was missing. He felt like shaking her. Instead, his hard features perceptibly darkened.

'O...kay,' he drawled cynically. 'Now share a shower with me,' he demanded with deliberate provocation, his fingers tightening on her arm.

Eloise was aware that Marcus was trying to rile her on purpose. Why, she had no idea. The only connection between them was sex, and from now on it was going to stay that way until their relationship had run to its natural conclusion, and without trust on either side that should not take too long. But for the moment she had to stay away from England; that was the most important thought in her head.

If she discovered she was unlucky enough to be pregnant, then all deals were off, KHE would have to get by without her, and she would be on her own. In the meantime, she would enjoy what Marcus offered. She could be as hard as a man, if she tried.

'Yes, okay.' She lifted her hand and placed it on his broad chest. 'Whatever you say.'

Marcus made love to her hard and fast with the water cascading over their naked bodies, he felt her climax, her fingernails tearing into his back as they both reached shattering fulfilment at the same time.

His breathing rough and audible, he shot her a blistering glance, and slowly unwound her long legs from around his waist and lowered her limp body to the floor. With one arm supporting her, he reached over and turned off the shower tap, then dropped a soft kiss on her forehead.

'We'd better get out of here and get dressed,' he said ruefully. 'I meant to tell you before I was distracted—Aunt Christine and Stella are coming for cocktails and dinner.'

Reeling under the force of her own response, to be hit with his relatives' arrival in pretty much the next breath simply confirmed for Eloise she had been right to decide emotional detachment was the only way to deal with Marcus.

Straightening, she shrugged off his arm. 'Right, okay,' she said calmly and, unconscious of her nudity, she stepped out of the shower. She picked a towel from the pile provided, wrapped it around her naked body and left the bathroom, without looking back at Marcus.

Okay—she had done it again... An incredulous frown pleating his broad brow, Marcus grabbed a towel and flung it around his hips. For the first time in his adult life he felt guilty about having sex, and he didn't like the feeling one bit.

Eloise quickly dried her body and slipped on her clothes without glancing in a mirror. She felt as if she was moving, talking, acting through a swirling fog. She had felt like this before and knew it was the shock of hearing the news about Rick Pritchard, and she had to battle to break free.

Only in Marcus's arms had she become truly aware again, a wry smile twisted her lips. Unfortunately, she couldn't spend the rest of the day in his arms. She knew from past experience it usually took about twenty-four hours for the paralysing fear to fade.

Dinner was not the ordeal Eloise had expected. Christine was a woman in her forties. She must have been Marcus's mum's younger sister, Eloise surmised. She was small and plump with gentle brown eyes, and Stella at seventeen was a younger version. It became increasingly apparent to Eloise as the meal progressed that Christine obviously had no knowledge of the state her husband had left his affairs in. She was a lovely lady and, from her comments to Marcus and to Eloise, it was obvious she had total and utter faith in Marcus to look after the financial side of her life.

After admiring the amber pendant Eloise was wearing and hearing Eloise worked as a jewellery designer, Christine remarked, 'You are the first girl my nephew has seen fit to introduce to our small family, and you are lucky. He is brilliant at business; he will help you.' She turned her warm brown eyes to Marcus. 'I am right. No?'

Eloise swallowed a lump in her throat at the expression of tender love they exchanged. And when the evening was over and Eloise stood at the door of the villa and was subjected to a hug and a kiss from Christine and Stella, plus a demand she must visit them for a meal, her throat closed up with emotion.

This would not do, she told herself, walking back inside. In any other circumstances she could have really loved Marcus's relatives... But the knowledge that her mother Chloe had had an affair with Christine's late husband and conned him out of a great deal of money made the bile rise in her throat and left her with an acrid taste on her tongue.

Meeting Christine had brought it home to her as nothing else could why Marcus held her in such low regard.

'Would you like a nightcap?' the object of her thoughts enquired as they entered the hall.

She arched her shapely brows. 'Not wise after all the wine I have consumed,' she responded flippantly. Actually, she hadn't drunk much, but she wanted to get away from Marcus for a while.

'Don't worry. I won't let you get drunk,' he advised her smoothly, his narrowed dark eyes skimming over her figure. Every shapely curve revealed by the green silk dress which was held up by tiny sequinned shoulder straps. It was so slim-fitting that there was a split up one side to enable her to walk, and he remembered the fun he had had buying it for her in Paris with a smile.

Eloise lifted a graceful shoulder. 'Yes, all right.'

His smile extinguished, Marcus's sensuous mouth tightened into a hard line. She looked at him and smiled, but it was as if she wasn't there. 'Sit on the terrace. I'll bring the drinks out,' he snapped. Without a word Eloise sat down and, instead of being pleased she had done as he said, Marcus felt irrationally angry.

Reclining on a lounger on the terrace with a glass of juice in her hand, Eloise glanced across at Marcus. He was leaning against the ornate balustrade, staring down at her. In a white dinner jacket and black trousers, he was devastatingly handsome, but the hint of anger glinting in the darkness of his eyes was unsettling. What had she done wrong now? she wondered bitterly. Not servile enough for him? Well, tough…

'You liked Christine and Stella?' Marcus prompted.

'Yes, they're both charming. In other circumstances I'm sure we could have been friends.'

'What do you mean—in other circumstances?' he demanded hardily. 'There is nothing wrong with now.'

Gracefully, Eloise rose to her feet and, after draining her glass, placed it on a nearby table.

'Okay, if you say so.'

'No, it is not damn well okay.' Marcus moved to block her path his hands closing like talons on her shoulders. 'What is with this "okay" to everything I say?' he growled with savage frustration. 'You've barely said a sentence since we left London.'

He hauled her against him and she looked up into his hard features, and was suddenly aware of the brush of his long body against her. 'Sorry, I didn't realise I was supposed to make brilliant conversation as part of our deal,' she said bluntly.

'Damn the deal, and talk to me,' Marcus groaned, his fingers gentling on her shoulders. 'This is my home, and I want you to be happy here.' His dark eyes caught and held her own. 'I want us to be happy here. Not just *okay*.' And as he said it he knew he meant it. He wanted much more from Eloise than sex. He wanted her warmth, her friendship, her *love*...

He wanted to forget their deal! Eloise was so surprised, the shock that had almost swamped her mind all day, but had begun to lift over dinner finally vanished, and she responded tentatively. 'I'm a bit tired from the flight and everything. Disorientated.'

Deep in her innermost being, she wanted to believe he was serious. She'd only ever belonged to Marcus in the physical sense, and with the warmth of his body enfolding her she was loath to give up the little he was prepared to give her. Was she going to let the ghost of the past that had haunted her all day win, or was she going to take one last chance?

'Let's go down to the beach,' Marcus suggested. 'The sea air will clear your head.'

'Ok—' She nearly said it again, and a brief smile tilted the corners of her mouth. 'A very good idea, I agree.'

Marcus slanted her a wry grin, and dropped an arm around her bare shoulders. 'Come on.'

They walked along the deserted beach in a relatively peaceful silence.

For Eloise the underlying tension was never far from the surface but, looking around her, scenting the clear night air, the only sound being the gentle movement of the sea, she realised she felt safe. She cast a sidelong glance at her companion through the thick fringe of her lashes, and knew she had Marcus to thank for her feeling of well-being, and she made a conscious decision to try and relax, live for the moment.

It was a wonderful night, a clear star-studded sky with the full moon gleaming on the dark water. Eloise kicked off her shoes and walked into the gentle waves whispering over the sand. The water was warm, and she turned play-fully back to Marcus. 'Come and have a paddle.'

'I can do better than that,' Marcus said thickly, and slowly he stripped off his jacket and spread it on the sand. His shirt, trousers, everything followed.

Astonished, wide-eyed, she watched her own personal striptease show, a slow burning need igniting in her belly. He stood tall and straight not a yard away. A work of art that rivalled Michaelangelo's David, perfect in line and form, and totally unashamed of his magnificent aroused body.

His dark eyes captured hers, and she was powerless to break the contact. 'Now it's your turn, Eloise.'

Hypnotised by the burning intensity of his gaze 'Yes,' she conceded softly. Safe and sure in his protection, she caught the hem of her dress; she slipped it over her head, and threw it onto the sand, freeing her high firm breasts to the warm night air and Marcus's rapacious, hungry and very masculine appraisal.

She tucked her fingers in the top of lacy white briefs, and slowly stepped out of them one leg at a time; then, straightening up, she squared her shoulders and looked at Marcus.

In silence they simply stared at each other, totally naked, at one with the earth, sea and sky.

Marcus reached out his hand, and Eloise placed her own small hand in his palm. His night-black eyes caught and held hers, the simmering passion in his gaze igniting her own. Adrenaline raced through her veins; anticipation heated her blood. For the first time in her life she rejoiced in her own sexuality, neither afraid nor ashamed.

In that moment she saw them as two supreme beings, naked as nature intended, free from all the shackles of convention, all worldly cares, and she stepped forward.

'You are perfection,' Marcus groaned as their mouths met in a desperate hungry passion.

He shaped her swollen breasts with shaking hands, his thumbs grazing over the hard tight peaks, before lifting her in his arms, and lying her on his outspread jacket. His large powerful body stretched out beside her his shoulders shook as he lifted his head. 'Every time I see you, I want you more.'

Reaching up Eloise framed his head in her hands and urged him down to her. 'Don't talk,' she murmured. She wanted nothing to spoil the erotic dream consuming her and pressed her mouth to his, her tongue daringly searching the moist depths of his mouth.

Time suspended in another dimension, they touched, tasted, and explored and, mindless in the grip of a primeval passion, the sea water gently lapping at their limbs, they finally came together in a glorious, slow-burning, ecstatic climax that left them both shuddering in the aftermath of exquisite pleasure.

Marcus recovered first and, smiling down at her, a smile of smug male satisfaction, he kissed the tip of her nose. 'Skinny-dipping next.'

It was another first for Eloise. She had never swum naked before and later, when they made their way back to the house, dishevelled and looking as if they had done exactly what they had done…she wondered if she ever would again.

The sun was shining through the window when Eloise's eyes fluttered open.

Marcus, a fully dressed Marcus, if one could call denim shorts and a sleeveless black tee-shirt fully dressed, was standing by the bed. 'What time is it, what are you doing?' she mumbled, closing her eyes again. So much virile male pulchritude was a jolt to her system so early in the morning.

'Almost noon.'

'What?' Her eyes flew open.

'I thought you needed the rest, and your friend Katy called. Apparently she has talked Harry into letting her come out for a few days. She will be arriving this afternoon.'

Her eyes properly open now, Eloise looked at Marcus. The lover of last night had gone; his dark eyes were narrowed speculatively on her small face, his body tense.

'That will be nice,' she said politely, his obvious reserve a timely reminder to her to keep her emotional distance from the man, and she dragged the cotton sheet up to her armpits.

'Maybe, but it seems rather a sudden decision on Katy's part,' Marcus opined darkly. 'So much so, I could be forgiven for thinking you had arranged it between you. Are you really that bored at the prospect of staying alone with me?'

His black eyes roamed broodingly over her beautiful face, the fabulous red hair spread over the pillow, to where she had tucked the sheet firmly across her breasts. His throat constricted as he recalled the lushness of her body beneath the sheet. Hell! What on earth was the matter with him? Challenging her like some jealous teenager, just because she had a friend coming to stay, when he wanted her all to himself, he finally acknowledged with a frown.

Watching him frown, Eloise shivered in spite of the heat. Marcus was back to his usual cool, remote self. Yet she could have sworn in the middle of the night she had felt his arms close around her, holding her close, protecting her. Sadly she realised it had been wishful thinking on her part. Inexplicably, she felt like crying but, gritting her teeth and fighting back the tears, she sat up in bed, pulling the sheet up under her chin.

Taking a deep breath, she tilted back her head. 'You have to be joking.' She forced a light laugh. 'I wouldn't dream of inviting a friend of mine anywhere near you, unless I had to. And may I point out this is your home; Katy asked you. You could have said no.' She knew she had gone too far; he took a step forward, his black eyes blazing, and then he stilled.

Marcus stared at her as if she had sprouted horns and a tail. Her words had cut deep. She had no family, but she didn't even want him near her friends, while he had wanted to bring her to his home, delighted in introducing her to his family, and was looking forward to her meeting his friends on the island.

In that moment, Marcus, a man who had never believed in love, suddenly realised he was madly, passionately in love with Eloise. He bent forward again. 'Eloise.' He had to tell her and, reaching out, he gently stroked her red hair from her face.

Eloise flinched back.

'No,' he said sharply. 'I…' and he could not say it. The deal, everything came flooding back, and he almost groaned out loud. How could he have been such a blind fool? He didn't give a damn about revenge. It was Eloise he wanted, had always wanted, and he'd been too arrogant, too jealous, to admit as much.

'I'll go and collect Katy,' he said, pulling back. 'You rest, eat, pamper yourself—do what women do.' He must sound like an incoherent idiot, he knew, but he had so much ground to make up with Eloise, he didn't know where to start.

A grim smile twisted his lips. He needed a strategy to woo her, win her love. On the plus side, he knew he wouldn't need to coerce her into bed. The chemistry between them was explosive. Maybe a private talk with Katy might give him a few pointers.

'Pamper?' Eloise exclaimed and, watching the fleeting expressions chase across his handsome face, she was totally confused.

Glancing back at Eloise, seeing the confusion in her emerald eyes, the master strategist lost it. 'I want us to stay together, get married, everything,' Marcus said with grim determination, sitting down on the bed and pulling her into his arms.

She shook her head, unable to believe her ears. He

looked more like he had swallowed a dose of horrible med-
icine than a suitor. Then he kissed her.

'Damn Katy,' Marcus muttered, lifting his head, as the
whirling blades of a helicopter landing broke the silence.

Eloise looked up and collided with lustrous dark eyes.
Was she dreaming or had Marcus really asked her to marry
him? He looked frustrated and, unbelievably for him, vulnerable, unsure. 'Katy,' she mumbled irrationally, too
stunned to comprehend what he meant.

'I have to go and collect her, but think about what I've
said,' he prompted, and leaping to his feet, he left.

Not for a moment admitting he had to get away, he was
as stunned as Eloise looked. He had proposed marriage
without a second thought. Hell, who was he kidding?
Without even a first thought! His brilliant mind had been
turned to mush by a pair of green eyes. Eloise drove him
crazy. He must be crazy to want to give up his freedom.
A few minutes after climbing into the waiting helicopter,
a broad smile broke on his face. He felt nothing but joy.

CHAPTER ELEVEN

'NO BENJAMIN with you?' Marcus asked, after the usual friendly greetings to Katy. 'I'm amazed you could bring yourself to leave him at home.' He smiled as he escorted the rather frazzled-looking Katy across the tarmac to the heliport. 'It must have been a sudden decision on your part to visit Eloise,' he prompted. He still had a lingering suspicion Eloise had somehow arranged this visit to avoid being alone with him, though he did not see how. He had never let Eloise out of his sight, since yesterday morning.

'It was, and I'm only staying the one night.' Katy shot him a worried frown. 'But after I read the newspaper, I really didn't think it was something I could tell Eloise over the phone.'

'Sounds dire. Don't tell me the firm has collapsed overnight without her,' Marcus quipped.

'No, but it does concern Eloise.' Katy glanced at Marcus, and was reassured by his cheerful grin.

'You know, before meeting you I would have bet Eloise would remain a virgin till her dying day,' she confided in him chattily. 'But she's blossomed incredibly into a confident woman with you to look after her. Harry and I were amazed when she agreed to go to that film premiere with you. I would have sworn Eloise would never appear in the public eye ever again after the trauma she went though with the court case. The victim's name is supposed to remain secret, but that slime-ball's letter from prison to the gutter press threatening revenge, nearly finished poor Eloise off. But your trip to the premiere convinced us both

she's finally got over her fear of men and recognition.'
Katy gave Marcus a grateful smile. 'But old habits die
hard; we've protected her for so long. I want to be there
for her when she finds out.'

Victim? Court case? His Eloise a virgin? Marcus's mind
reeled under the implication, a deep, dark, bottomless pit
opening up before him. Katy obviously thought he knew
what she was talking about. Glancing up, he realised they
were at the helicopter.

'Finds out what?' he asked lightly, helping Katy into the
helicopter and handing her a set of headphones, desperate
to continue the conversation in flight.

'This is great. I've never been in a helicopter before.'

Marcus forced a smile at Katy, but he had to know why
she was here. Something was terribly wrong. 'Yes, but you
were going to tell me...'

'Oh, yes.' Katy sobered. 'Eloise will have told you all
about the assault and stabbing.' Marcus felt the blood drain
from his face, and he listened in growing horror as Katy
rambled on.

'It was a terrible time, and she was so brave all through
the trial. But what you can't know—I only found out late
last night, when I got around to reading the paper—Rick
Pritchard, the man who attacked her, who got a seven-year
sentence, is to be released on Monday after serving only
four years.'

'I see.' Marcus froze, the blood turning to ice in his
veins.

'Yes, well, after he was sentenced, he vowed from the
dock he would get Eloise, and I saw the look in the fiend's
eyes. I wouldn't put anything past him. The letter he sent
to a newspaper a couple of weeks later simply reaffirmed
the fact. But she has you to protect her and the fact she's
in Greece instead of London is actually quite fortuitous.

The swine is unlikely to find her on Rykos,' Katy opined, ending on a cheerful note. 'Oh, look, I can see the sea and dozens of little islands. It's beautiful.'

'Yes.' Marcus carefully pointed out various landmarks. He did not dare reopen the discussion on the attack. He had never felt such rage and fury in his life, or such disgust, most of it directed at himself. God, what had he done? Suddenly a lot of little things made sense. Katy's and Harry's protectiveness towards Eloise; Eloise's dislike of publicity—and he silently groaned.

The sound of the helicopter made Eloise's heart skip a beat. They were back. With one last glance in the mirror, she ran from the bedroom, and down the stairs, happy anticipation giving a bloom to her cheeks, and brilliance to her emerald eyes.

She wasn't dreaming; Marcus had asked her to marry him. The why and wherefore she would have to discuss with him but, for the first time since meeting Marcus again, her heart was bursting with hope for the future. She'd told herself not to get too excited but she couldn't help it. She'd dressed in a simple mint sheath dress, and on her feet she wore soft leather mules in the same colour. She had brushed her hair back and left it loose. She didn't want to overdo it and look as if she had dressed up especially for Marcus.

Stopping her dash for the door, she made herself walk slowly out on the terrace and around to the rear of the house, in sight of the landing pad. She watched as the tall figure of Marcus stepped down from the helicopter and swung the smaller figure of Katy to the ground.

'Fantastic,' Katy murmured, walking around the terrace with Marcus at her side, and the houseman bringing up the rear, carrying Katy's holdall. 'This is some house, Eloise!'

'Glad you like it.' Eloise grinned at Katy. 'Wait until you see the pool,' and she glanced up at Marcus. 'Perhaps we can all try it later when Katy's settled.' She smiled a little nervously, still a bit unsure about his proposal, but there was no reciprocal smile; his dark features looked coldly remote.

'Not for me. I have some work to do in my study. Nikos here will show you Katy's room, and as she is only staying one night I'm sure you two want to gossip. I'll see you both at dinner.' He strode into the shadowed interior of the house without a backward glance.

One phone call and Marcus turned pale as death. The hand holding the receiver shook with the force of his emotions. 'Fax me the lot—trial transcript, newspaper articles, everything.' Dropping the phone, he paced the length of his study like a caged tiger.

He couldn't believe it, didn't want to, but he knew it was true. When the fax machine started printing he sat down at his desk and started to read. The detective he had hired had said before Eloise was as *pure as the driven snow* and he, with his cynical mind, had thought he was being facetious. To see it in black and white in the trial transcript made him sick to his stomach. She had been a virgin when she was attacked, and technically still had been afterwards. The fiend had not succeeded.

Eloise, his Eloise, had been returning across a park alone after a game of tennis, and been brutally attacked by a depraved man, Rick Pritchard. Luckily a couple out walking their dog had disturbed him. Eloise had been rushed to hospital and the police called, and then the stab-wound to her inner thigh had been treated and she'd regained consciousness.

He buried his head in his hands, the full horror of what had happened to Eloise piercing him like a knife in the heart. The scar on her leg... She had said it was an accident. She had nearly bled to death...

Leaping to his feet, he wanted to smash something, or someone; impotent fury blazed in his black eyes. He had never felt such rage, such hatred, in his life; he wanted to kill Rick Pritchard with his bare hands. That being impossible, he once more picked up the phone. There was not a flicker of emotion in his dark sardonic features, but the implacable intent in his jet-black eyes would have scared the devil himself, as in a cold, hard voice he issued his instructions.

'A lovely pad,' Katy declared half an hour later seated opposite Eloise at the small table on the balcony of her bedroom. Nikos had thoughtfully provided a jug of iced tea and two glasses, plus a plate of various Greek delicacies to nibble on.

'I can see why Marcus wanted to bring you here, you lucky girl.' She sighed in delight at the panoramic view of sea and sky.

Eloise looked across at her friend. 'Okay, Katy, why the rush out here?' It was totally out of character for Katy to fly anywhere unless she had to.

Bright brown eyes turned compassionately to Eloise. 'There's no easy way of saying this. Rick Pritchard is due to be released from jail on Monday.'

Eloise quelled an internal shiver at the mention of the name. She should have guessed. She'd read the article in the paper herself yesterday morning. Of course Katy must have seen it and, being Katy, worried over her.

'Is that all?' Eloise tried a smile, deeply touched by Katy's concern. But if the last few months had taught her anything, it was she could no longer hide from the harsh reality of life or depend on other people to protect her.

Katy had her own family and life to lead. 'I know, Katy. I saw the article when you gave me the paper yesterday. It is not important,' she lied.

'You're sure? You're not frightened he'll come after you?' Katy asked seriously.

'Really, Katy... Do I look frightened?' Eloise prompted and, casually picking up a small stuffed vine leaf, she waved her hand around. 'Look where we are and with whom. Marcus is more than a match for any man, or woman!' She allowed a brief, knowing smile to curve her lips, before she popped the morsel of food in her mouth.

'Yes, you're right.' Katy smiled back, completely taken in by Eloise's consummate acting. 'Harry said I was worrying unnecessarily, and Marcus seemed quite cool when I told him about it. But, hey, now I am here, can we at least try out the pool.'

The food stuck in Eloise's throat and she had to swallow hard to dislodge it horrified by Katy's comment. 'You told Marcus?'

'Yes, on the way over. Why, does it matter?'

Recovering swiftly. 'No. No, of course not, but do me a favour—don't mention it to him again.' The thought of Marcus knowing her dark secret mortified her. 'He's Greek, a typical macho male, and as you can imagine any mention of an attack on his lady puts him in a bad mood.' She made it up as she went along. 'And I really don't want to talk about the case.'

But she knew she was only putting off the moment of reckoning. Once Marcus got her on her own he would want the full story. Now she understood why he had appeared cold on his return with Katy.

'Sure, if you say so. The subject's closed,' Katy said understandingly, then grinned. 'Now lead me to the water.'

They spent the rest of the afternoon at the pool, but there

was no sign of Marcus. The whole situation put Eloise under a severe strain. So far, by some miracle she had managed to fool Katy into thinking Marcus was the love of her life and everything was fine. If Katy realised everything was not as it seemed, she would question Eloise until she got the truth.

But what was the truth? Eloise thought as she stood in the bedroom, fastening polished jade earrings to her ears, a perfect match for the patterned green silk sarong-style dress she had opted to wear for dinner. So much had happened, so fast. She was plunged into turmoil by her conflicting emotions.

Yesterday morning she had told herself she hated Marcus, because he'd ordered her to come to Greece, but after reading the newspaper she'd jumped at the chance to get away. She'd spent all day in a state of shock. Then last night and the episode on the beach when she had succumbed to his blatant sexuality yet again, she'd felt no shame, but freedom. This morning Marcus had asked her to marry him, and for a while she'd believed happiness was a possibility. But when he returned with Katy, it was as if the last twenty-four hours had never happened.

Dear heaven, it was no wonder she was an emotional basket case, she told herself bitterly. She was a complete novice when it came to male-female relationships, and Marcus was a vastly experienced, complicated man. He was also a very traditional male, with a high profile position to uphold in the business world. Not the sort of man who would take for his wife a woman who had been violated and the centre of a sordid court case, she concluded sadly.

Straightening her shoulders, she left the room to collect Katy and go down to dinner, her stomach churning with nervous dread, waiting for the axe to fall. Trying to understand what drove Marcus was like riding a roller-coaster, a spectacular high then a deep, depressing trough. Never mind the fact some madman might be chasing her...

They ate dinner out on the terrace with the sea and night sky as a backdrop. Marcus looked his usual magnificent self in a lightweight linen suit, and by the coffee stage he had shed his jacket. He ruled the conversation with all the charm and wit of a true Renaissance man. Katy was completely fooled, but Eloise could sense the underlying tension in the taut set of his wide shoulders.

She hadn't had a private word with him since his bombshell proposal this morning. He'd waited until she and Katy had appeared for dinner before exiting his study with a murmured apology about changing for dinner. He was avoiding her, obviously disgusted.

Now, the few times their eyes met, his narrowed into hard darkness masking all expression. Obviously he was regretting his reckless proposal, Eloise thought sadly, but then she had not really believed him anyway. Miracles didn't happen. At least not to her.

Inwardly she heaved a sigh of relief when, after demolishing almost a whole bottle of wine single-handedly, Katy said she was tired and wanted to go to bed.

'Yes. I'm rather tired myself,' Eloise agreed, rising from her seat. She glanced across at Marcus. 'I think I'll call it a night,' she said smoothly, playing her part for the benefit of Katy. 'If you don't mind.' Her green eyes widened as she saw the flash of something almost feral in the black eyes that met her own.

'You do that, sweetheart,' he said. With perfect manners, he rose as they did, and turning to Katy wished her good night, and then, glancing at Eloise, he added, 'I am going to have a brandy. I will see *you* later.'

Following Katy into the house, Eloise heard the sarcasm

in his tone, and slanted him a sharp backward glance—but, to her astonishment, she caught an expression of such bitter devastation on his darkly handsome face, her step paused. She wanted to go to him and ask him what was wrong. Then common sense prevailed; she was imagining things. Marcus had never needed anyone in his life, and she caught up with Katy, and showed her to her room.

Shedding her clothes, Eloise showered, and slipped a brief white cotton nightgown over her head. Returning to the bedroom, brush in hand, she sat down on the bed, and began brushing her hair. Marcus confused and tormented her, until she could no longer think straight. She'd tried. She'd tried to retain some control, to defend her poor heart against the overwhelming attraction of the man, but she was beginning to believe it was a hopeless task. She was hopeless. Her lower lip trembled; a solitary tear rolled down her cheek, and she brushed it away with her free hand, then brushed her hair with more ferocity than was strictly necessary. She refused to wallow in self-pity; she was a survivor—she had proved that once before, and she could do so again.

Lost in her own thoughts, Eloise did not know how long she had been sitting on the bed, when she glanced up and saw Marcus standing a few feet away.

He was as cold and still as a marble statue. She could see it in his eyes, feel it in the silence. Eloise swallowed hard vaguely threatened by his silent scrutiny. 'The bathroom's free,' she said inanely.

'So is your attacker,' Marcus hissed between clenched teeth. 'Why didn't you tell me you'd been attacked?' he demanded softly.

'I didn't think you'd be interested. Anyway, Katy has told you now,' Eloise answered bluntly, staring at him as he wrenched off his tie as if it were choking him and undid the first few buttons of his shirt.

'Katy thought I knew,' he raked at her, tight-lipped with temper. 'After a few calls, I finally received the transcript of the trial and the press reports. I have just finished reading them.'

All the colour drained from Eloise's face, and the brush fell unnoticed from her hand to the bed. 'It was a long time ago,' she tried to say nonchalantly, but the tremble in her voice was plain to hear. She hated the thought of Marcus reading every horrible torturous intimate detail of the worst episode in her life.

'Why didn't you tell me?' Marcus demanded savagely. 'Why did you lie? I asked you about your scar and you said it had been caused by an accident.'

Eloise slowly stood up, and told him the truth. 'I was shy; it was the first... I didn't want you to know, not then, but later maybe.'

'Why, why in God's name would you hide such a thing from me?' Marcus's fury was so real she took a nervous step back. He saw it, and went white, strain etched in every line of his face. He had thought she was a virgin, but had ignored it, and it only served to make him more furious. 'You were afraid of me.' He hissed in outraged disbelief.

Eloise shivered. 'No, I just wanted to forget.'

'Forget?' he bit out incredulously, 'And how the hell am I supposed to forget?' Marcus seethed, his glittering black eyes clashing with hers, and she caught her breath. She did not have to listen to this. It was as she had thought—he was disgusted by the court case, disgusted with her.

'The exquisite face, the luscious body.' His gaze slid down over her scantily-clad form and he reached out and caught her wrist as she would have whirled away.

'God, but you've got your revenge, Eloise.' He surveyed her with burning intensity. 'Have you the slightest idea how I feel? How can I forget that I all but forced you into my bed?' he demanded, his black eyes raking over her with contempt.

Eloise flinched as though she had been struck, but pride alone made her face him. She stiffened, and stared at him with ice-green eyes. Another room, another man accusing her. As if it was her fault she was a beautiful sexy girl, a tease—of course she led the defendant on. It was the past come back to haunt her yet again.

'Don't touch me. Let go of my arm,' Eloise snapped, cold anger covering the pain he was inflicting by his callous words. 'If, as you say, you read the transcript, you know that technically it was attempted rape and assault with a deadly weapon. You do not come into that category.' Eloise threw him a look of pure scorn, denying the feelings he could arouse in her even when he was behaving like the worst kind of chauvinist. 'Yet,' she concluded viciously.

Marcus released her so abruptly she fell back against the bed. He lifted his hand and drove shaking fingers through his thick hair. Hell, what was he doing, raging at Eloise? None of this was her fault. She was the victim, and he was filled with self-contempt.

'I shouldn't have said that,' he conceded tautly. 'I allowed my anger to get the better of me. Sorry.'

She raised her eyes. Marcus saying sorry was a new experience—but one look at his face and she realised he looked less in command of himself than usual. In fact he looked absolutely dreadful. 'Forget it,' Eloise muttered with a negative shake of her head, and sat down on the bed, her trembling legs no longer capable of supporting her. 'I have.' After the court case, she'd vowed never to be forced by any man into defending her actions, and she was not about to do so now with Marcus.

There was a long silence, then Marcus took a deep breath and straightened to his full height. 'I can't forget what that man did to you Eloise. I wasn't angry with you, I was furious with him, and myself.' His black eyes captured hers, and there was no doubt of the sincerity in their depths. 'I feel like the lowest of the low. I refused to believe a word you said, because all the evidence made you seem a liar. So I didn't care how I got you in my bed, as long as I did. I would be lying if I said I regretted making love to you—I don't, though I recognise I'm not much better than the man who attacked you. But you have nothing to fear from me, Eloise; I will never touch you again.'

Eloise turned paper-white, and there was an even longer silence while she digested what he'd said, and stared back at him, her green eyes curiously blank. She had been a challenge to him, but he didn't want her any more.

'It's okay,' she said finally. She had always suspected once he discovered her past he would lose interest in her. 'I'll go back with Katy tomorrow.' She wasn't going to cry, she wasn't going to beg. 'As for the money I owe...'

'You don't owe me a thing, Eloise. I've known that since Harry told me how you'd invested your inheritance to start the business and you're all equal partners that you don't care about money.'

Eloise knew somewhere in the back of her mind he was telling her something vital, but she couldn't think straight. She felt sick inside and, taking a few deep breaths, it was only by a mighty effort of will she managed to shore up the defensive wall in her mind that stopped her bawling her eyes out. 'Okay.'

She was doing it again. Marcus's dark eyes narrowed, harsh and brooding, on her pale face and finally his brilliant brain discerned instantly what she was doing. He was appalled he hadn't recognised the tactic sooner, appalled at his own insensitivity.

'No, damn it, it is not *okay*,' he swore. 'Don't do that again. I realise now why you were like that yesterday. You were in shock; it's self-protection. You knew, didn't you? You knew the rat was being set free.'

'I read the paper before we left London. Yes,' she admitted, her head bent, no longer caring what Marcus thought or felt. Just wishing he would leave, before she broke down completely.

A deep agonised groan had her lifting her head. Marcus stood, shoulders stooped, his hands covering his face, and as she watched his hands slid down to his sides. He stared down at her, his black eyes glazed with moisture, his handsome features twisted in horror.

'What is it, Marcus?' she asked hoarsely, deeply disturbed by his ashen pallor.

'God help me!' His tormented black eyes caught and held hers. 'Yesterday you were in shock and I ordered you into the shower.'

Eloise had never seen such pain and anguish in her life, and slowly it dawned on her—Marcus, her arrogant, infuriating, powerful lover, the keeper of her heart if he did but know it, was racked with guilt.

She reached up and placed her hand on his curled fist. 'I enjoyed our sojourn in the shower,' she said softly.

He continued to stare at her for a disturbing length of time, as if he had not heard; then his fist unfurled and he clasped her hand in a deathlike grip. 'Oh, God, Eloise,' he groaned from deep in his throat, and pulled her up into his arms, crushing her to him. 'I wish that were true.'

'It is,' she murmured tilting back her head to look up into his agonised face.

He stared at her for a moment in solemn silence, his eyes probing hers with a burning intensity; then, as if he could not help himself, he groaned again, his dark head descending. 'I love you so much, Eloise.' He buried his face against her throat. 'I can't bear the thought of anyone hurting you, and I know I must have hurt you. God! I took your innocence, I made you stay with me. I am no better than the scum who stabbed you.'

She felt as if all the air had left her lungs, by the fierce pressure of his arms, and she couldn't believe what she was hearing. Her mouth fell open in shock. Marcus loved her. She lifted a tentative hand to his head. She hated to see her proud, arrogant lover so distraught, and she knew what she had to do.

'Marcus, you never hurt me, and certainly not physically. I always wanted you, even when we fought. I want you to believe me.'

'You are too soft-hearted for your own good,' he groaned against her throat and, lifting his head, his black eyes lingered on her slightly parted lips. 'You need someone to take care of you,' and he brushed his mouth over hers in the lightest of kisses. 'Let it be me, and I swear no one will ever hurt you again.'

'You...you love me?' She had to ask, to be sure.

'Eloise,' he murmured thickly, his fingers brushing her hair lightly from her flushed cheeks, while his eyes devoured her. 'I love you, and I have never felt more unworthy than I do at this moment. I can only pray that you will forgive me and let me try to make you happy.'

Her green eyes widened to their fullest extent as he spoke; it was almost too incredible to believe, but it was there in the gleaming depths of his dark eyes. It was there in the arms that tightened around her almost in desperation, and she finally knew it was there in his heart. 'There is nothing to forgive,' she whispered unsteadily. 'Just kiss me and tell me again you love me.'

He kissed her with a tender passion that stirred her more deeply than anything had ever done before. Her arms linked around his neck and she lost herself in the miracle of the moment.

'I love you, Eloise,' Marcus groaned and, sweeping her off her feet, laid her down on the bed, removing her nightgown in between kisses. He stared down at her and, with a hand that visibly shook, he traced the length of her leg and the hard ridge of tissue. For a second his dark eyes flashed violently. 'God, I could kill him,' he snarled.

'Marcus.' She held out her arms to him. 'Forget him and come to me.'

He made love to her with a care a depth of passion that touched her soul. His mouth found the scar and laved the length, and more. Eloise held nothing back and gave as much pleasure as she received, until they lay sated in each other's arms, two hearts beating as one perfect whole.

'Please marry me,' Marcus rasped throatily, and Eloise moved sinuously against him.

'Another deal?' she teased, glancing up at the darkly handsome face above her, and was stunned by the vulnerability in his night black eyes.

'No.' His sensuous mouth tightened. 'You never were, or were never meant to be.' Marcus said with scrupulous honesty. 'We need to talk.' Rolling onto his side, he propped his head on one hand and looked down at her.

'When Theo died, and I discovered what Chloe had done, I hired a detective to find her. When I was informed Chloe was dead and she had no sister, I was intrigued. The money meant little to me; I was more interested in finding you, to be brutally honest,' he said ruefully. 'You had haunted my dreams for years, seriously curbed my womanising ways, and I was curious to discover what had become of you.'

'I don't think I like the womaniser bit.' Eloise grinned up at him, but the rest was like manna to her love-starved heart.

'Yes, well, when the detective found you and informed me of your real name, and you owned a jewellery firm, I was bitterly disappointed; along with the signature on the contract it seemed to confirm that you were in league with Chloe. Then, when the detective told me you were as pure as the driven snow, I didn't want to hear any more. In my cynical mind, I thought he was being sarcastic. I decided to look you up, and come to some arrangement over what I considered should be Theo's share.'

'But I told you the truth, Marcus. My mother used my college project and she also forged my signature. It had absolutely nothing to do with me,' Eloise protested.

'I know that now.' Marcus calmed her with a finger across her lips. 'Let me finish. When I saw you by chance at the supper club, I was struck dumb; you were more beautiful than I remembered, and you were with a much older man.'

'I wasn't *with* Ted, well…'

'Shh. For the first time in my life I was hit by jealousy. And I thought of what you and your mother had done to my uncle and his family—and I was furious.'

'I told you….'

His dark head swooped and he stopped her with a kiss. 'Please, Eloise, I want to get everything out in the open between us. No more secrets.

'When I took you out to dinner, I was going to expose you as a liar and a cheat and demand Theo's money back—but, over the meal, you were so sweet, so much fun, I thought, why bother? I didn't need the money, and then, when we made love...'

Eloise smiled dreamily up at him. 'That night was so perfect. It was a miracle for me. I never expected to be able to let a man touch me, but with you it was different. I think it was because I had known you before the attack, and so you weren't a stranger. It was as though the trauma of the past didn't exist and I was nineteen again.'

His dark eyes locked with hers. 'God, Eloise! What I have put you though?' he said slowly, and she felt his muscles lock with tension. 'I know it was your first time. You were so nervous, so obviously inexperienced. I fully intended to keep on seeing you, and to forget about the fraud against my uncle.

'Then, after the phone call, when we were leaving, and you quite happily said you had obtained finance from Ted Charlton the night before. Everything you said suggested you'd slept with him. You got back to your apartment at three. You were so excited it was five before you finally slept—I wanted to strangle you. Then you signed the deal in the morning and celebrated over lunch.' His dark eyes clouded with remembered pain. 'I was gutted, thinking I must have been mistaken about your innocence, as you had spent the night and half the day with Ted to get him to invest in KHE, just like your mother, and then came to me.'

'You...' Amazement made her eyes widen. 'You actually... I wondered why you were so dismissive when you took me home.' Eloise stared at him. 'But it was nothing like that! Ted left me at the door. When I said *we* discussed Paris, I meant Katy, Harry and I. They waited up for me, as they tend to worry over me since the attack. Ted called the next day for a meeting with Harry, and then took us all out to lunch.' Recalling the conversation at the time,

Eloise realised how it might have sounded. 'But if you thought… No wonder…' she trailed off.

A wry smile twisted his sensuous lips. 'That's exactly what I thought. My ego took an absolute hammering; I didn't know if I was on my head or my heels. I needed to get away from you, to think.'

'I don't like the sound of that,' Eloise murmured, wriggling a little closer to the warmth of his naked body.

He chuckled and continued. 'I delayed going to America, and deliberately took Nadine to the charity ball, hoping you would see the photograph.'

'I did,' Eloise admitted. 'I was terribly hurt but, funnily enough, in one way I was grateful, because even if I never saw you again, you had cured me of my emotional hang-up where men were concerned. At least, that was what I told myself.'

One dark brow arched sardonically. 'I'll take that as a compliment—but I'm not sure I want to be seen as a sex counsellor.'

Eloise gave him a playful punch in the chest and let her hand linger there lovingly. 'You'd better not, Buster. I'm the only female you're ever going to counsel.'

'You're the only female I want to.' He ran a tender hand down her throat and over the soft swell of her breast.

She shivered and covered his hand with her own. 'And Nadine, what happened to her?' she asked hesitantly.

'I'm a lot older than you are, and there have been women in my life—but only on a casual basis. Nadine was one of them. I hadn't seen her for some months and I looked her up when I arrived in London, but that was as far as it went. Our first date and I saw you and no other woman would do. You're the only woman I have slept with since the moment I saw you again. Believe me.'

She wanted to believe him, and she knew some things

she would have to take on trust. 'I do.' But she still didn't understand why he hadn't come back for three months, and she asked him.

A dull tide of red ran up over his high cheekbones, and he looked less than his usual arrogant self. 'I didn't dare. But, God, I wanted to... Haven't you realised yet? You're my obsession, you drive me crazy. I love you quite desperately. After making love to you, there could never be anyone else for me. When I went to America—' he hesitated '—I was so angry, I was determined I was going to make you pay. I consulted my lawyer, supposedly on behalf of Aunt Christine, and he was of the opinion the legal case would cost more than the actual money Theo had lost, and that an out-of-court settlement was the way to go. But I told myself I didn't want to see you ever again, and I tried, I really tried. I concentrated on work to the exclusion of all else, determined to forget you ever existed. Then Ted Charlton got in touch with me and almost begged me to take over his commitment to KHE. After two months of aching for you, I thought, why not? It was a legitimate reason for seeing you. Then he told me he had slept with you, and confirmed what I suspected. All my anger surged back, a hundred times worse. I convinced myself if you slept with him for money, you could damn well sleep with me.'

It was Eloise's turn to put her finger over his lips. 'I really never slept with him.'

His mouth quirked in self-derision. 'I know that. I think I've always known, but jealousy is a powerful emotion. And, if I'm honest, deep down you terrified me; it suited me to think of you as some kind of thief, because then I could deny the very real feelings I had for you. I could pretend you were just like all the other women I have known, self-seeking and greedy. If I once admitted you

were different, I knew my bachelor days would be num-
bered. I told myself I was buying into KHE to help Ted
and to get Theo's money back, but I came to the opening
of the Paris boutique, secretly hoping you would...' He
lifted an elegant bronzed shoulder. 'I don't know...fall at
my feet in love and gratitude,' he said wryly.

Eloise half smiled. His description was not far wrong;
she very nearly had.

'It wasn't funny,' Marcus murmured intently, brushing
a caressing hand gently over her firm breast, as if compelled. 'I ached to be like this with you again, but instead
you looked at me like something you would scrape off the
bottom of your shoe.'

Eloise sighed, stirring against him, and grinned. 'That
bad, hmm?'

This confession was certainly good for *her* soul, but she
wasn't so sure it was doing much for Marcus's ego. 'But
you blackmailed me into your bed anyway,' she prompted
him.

'By then I was determined to have you, and Ted had
given me the lever, and to my shame I used it. Revenge
is a very powerful emotion and I figured you owed my
family.'

'So when did you finally realise you loved me?' She
tried to sit up, and Marcus held her back down by simply
rolling over her, his elbows either side of her shoulders
and his hands cupping her head. The fully naked body
contact and the warmth of his breath on her face made her
lose her train of thought for a second.

A long kiss later, he stared into her emerald eyes. 'I
always have; I was going to marry you when you were
nineteen, but you vanished. So I denied I loved you to
myself. I thought it was a sign of weakness, and I kept on
denying it.' A dull tide of colour washed over his olive

skin. 'Until this morning, I looked at you and I knew I was fooling no one but myself. My control snapped and I probably made the least romantic marriage proposal known to man, and I dared not wait to hear your answer in case it was no.'

'I liked it.'

'Forgive me, Eloise, and marry me.' She was stunned to see a trace of doubt in his night-black eyes. 'I will look after you, protect you, and I know I can make you love me eventually or die trying.'

'You won't have to try. I do love you, Marcus, and the answer is yes.'

EPILOGUE

KATY collapsed on to the bamboo cane sofa next to Harry. 'Let the holiday begin; give me a drink quick.'

Eloise smiled and Marcus stood up and crossed to the drinks trolley. 'What will it be, Katy—wine or something stronger?'

'G and T. I need it.'

With a sigh of contentment, Eloise watched her husband of a month mix the drink. They had married in a simple ceremony in the island church, with close friends and family, plus every inhabitant of the island. Eloise had never been happier.

Her sparkling emerald eyes followed Marcus; he never failed to stir her. This evening he was wearing tailored shorts and a soft cotton shirt, and he was without doubt the most handsome sexiest man alive, and he loved her.

As if sensing her scrutiny, he handed Katy the glass and crossed to sit down next to her, slipping an arm around her shoulder, and squeezing gently. 'All right, my love?' he enquired huskily and, running the tip of his tongue along her pouting lips, he claimed them with a kiss.

'Never better,' she whispered back, her pulse speeding up, and for a moment wished she had not invited Katy and Harry to stay for a week.

'You two are hopeless,' Harry teased. 'We came here on holiday, not to watch an X-rated show.'

Leaning back, Marcus chuckled. 'Well, we are all adults here.' Glancing with mocking intent around the terrace he added, 'The little devil Benjamin has finally gone to bed, it seems.'

'Yes, thank God.' Katy sighed, taking a long swallow of her G and T.

'I don't suppose you've heard yet,' Harry said, changing the subject. 'It was in the paper last week; Rick Pritchard apparently got into a fight outside a pub in Dover. He was found in a back alley, badly beaten, and is now in intensive care. They reckon it was foreigners, probably illegal immigrants that did it, because they've all vanished. So you won't have to worry about him any more.'

'I never did worry about him,' Marcus said smoothly. 'His sort usually get what they deserve.'

Watching Marcus, Eloise had the strangest feeling he was not the least surprised by the news.

Later when they were alone in their bedroom, she leant against him, her hand toying with the waistband of his briefs. 'Did you know about Pritchard?' she asked huskily, her own breathing unsteady, as his hands slid up under the fine silk of her nightgown to curve around her bottom, urging her closer.

'I would die if I lost you.' Marcus groaned as her fingers traced the hard masculine length of him.

'That's no answer,' she murmured unsteadily, glancing up and catching a flash of something that looked suspiciously like triumph in her indomitable husband's eyes.

'It's the only one you need,' Marcus growled and, sweeping off her nightgown, he carried her to the bed.

And he was right. Eloise sighed happily some time later, safe in his arms.

The world's bestselling romance series.

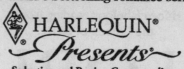

HARLEQUIN®
Presents

Seduction and Passion Guaranteed!

A new trilogy by **Carole Mortimer**

Three cousins of Scottish descent—they're male, millionaires and marriageable!

Meet Logan, Fergus and Brice, three tall, dark, handsome men-about-town. They've made their millions in London, but their hearts belong to the heather-clad hills of their grandfather's Scottish estate.

Logan, Fergus and Brice are about to give up their keenly fought-for bachelor status for three wonderful women. Laugh, cry and read all about their trials and tribulations in their pursuit of love.

Look out for:
To Marry McCloud
On sale August, #2267

Coming next month:
To Marry McAllister
On sale September, #2273

Pick up a Harlequin Presents novel and you will enter a world of spine-tingling passion and provocative, tantalizing romance!

HARLEQUIN®
Makes any time special®

Available wherever Harlequin books are sold.

Visit us at www.eHarlequin.com

HPBACH3

More fabulous reading from
the Queen of Sizzle!

LORI
FOSTER

with

Forever and Always

Back by popular demand are the scintillating stories of
Gabe and Jordan Buckhorn. They're gorgeous, sexy
and single…at least for now!

Available wherever books are sold—September 2002.

And look for Lori's *brand-new* single title,
CASEY in early 2003

HARLEQUIN®
Makes any time special ®

Visit us at www.eHarlequin.com

PHLF-2

Harlequin invites you to experience the charm and delight of

C O O P E R ' S   C O R N E R

A brand-new continuity
starting in August 2002

HIS BROTHER'S BRIDE
by *USA Today* bestselling author
Tara Taylor Quinn

Check-in: TV reporter Laurel London and noted travel writer William Byrd are guests at the new Twin Oaks Bed and Breakfast in Cooper's Corner.

Checkout: William Byrd suddenly vanishes and while investigating, Laurel finds herself face-to-face with policeman Scott Hunter. Scott and Laurel face a painful past. Can cop and reporter mend their heartbreak and get to the bottom of William's mysterious disappearance?

HARLEQUIN®
Makes any time special®

Visit us at www.cooperscorner.com

CC-CNM1R

Harlequin Presents®
and
Harlequin Romance®
have come together to celebrate a year of royalty

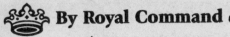 **By Royal Command**

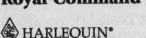 HARLEQUIN®
Romance®

EMOTIONALLY EXHILARATING!

Coming in June 2002
His Majesty's Marriage, #3703
Two original short stories by Lucy Gordon and Rebecca Winters

On-sale July 2002
The Prince's Proposal, #3709
by Sophie Weston

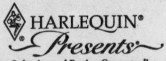 HARLEQUIN®
Presents

Seduction and Passion Guaranteed!

Coming in August 2002
Society Weddings, #2268
Two original short stories by Sharon Kendrick and Kate Walker

On-sale September 2002
The Prince's Pleasure, #2274
by Robyn Donald

**Escape into the exclusive world of royalty with
our royally themed books**

Available wherever Harlequin books are sold.

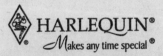 HARLEQUIN®
Makes any time special®

Visit us at www.eHarlequin.com

HPRROY

The world's bestselling romance series.

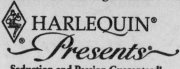

HARLEQUIN®
Presents

Seduction and Passion Guaranteed!

**Harlequin Presents®
invites you to escape into
the exclusive world of royalty
with our royally themed books**

By Royal Command

Look out for:
The Prince's Pleasure
by **Robyn Donald**, #2274
On sale September 2002

**Pick up a Harlequin Presents® novel
and you will enter a world of
spine-tingling passion and
provocative, tantalizing romance!**

Available wherever Harlequin books are sold.

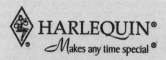

HARLEQUIN®
Makes any time special ®

Visit us at www.eHarlequin.com

HPRC

Coming Next Month

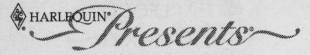

HARLEQUIN *Presents*

THE BEST HAS JUST GOTTEN BETTER!

#2271 AN ARABIAN MARRIAGE Lynne Graham
The first book in Lynne's Sister Brides trilogy, this story is
dramatic, passionate and deeply emotional—it has it all! When
Crown Prince Jaspar al-Husayn bursts into her life, Freddy realizes he
has come to take their nephew away. Refusing to part with the child
she loves, she proposes marriage to Jaspar!

#2272 ETHAN'S TEMPTRESS BRIDE Michelle Reid
The second Hot-Blooded Husbands book is a unique and
compelling story with vibrant characterization and hot, hot
sensuality! Millionaire businessman Ethan Hayes told himself that Eve
was a spoiled little rich girl, intent on bringing men to their knees. But
it was all he could do to resist the temptation....

#2273 TO MARRY McALLISTER Carole Mortimer
Read the final title in the Bachelor Cousins trilogy and witness
the Scottish hero trading his independence for romance!
Dangerously attractive Brice McAllister has been commissioned to
paint a portrait of supermodel Sabina Smith. Aware of their mutual
attraction, he moves the sitting to a romantic, remote castle in Scotland....

#2274 THE PRINCE'S PLEASURE Robyn Donald
Part of the miniseries By Royal Command, this book celebrates
our year of royalty with an exclusive wedding! Prince Luka of
Dacia trusts nothing and no one—least of all his unexpected desire for
Alexa. Torn between passion and privacy, Luka commands that Alexa
stay safely behind closed doors entirely for his pleasure....

#2275 THE HIRED HUSBAND Kate Walker
An unusual, fascinating and very sexy marriage-of-convenience
story. You'll love the gorgeous hero!
Sienna Rushford desperately needs to claim her inheritance—
but her father's will states she must be happily married! So she hires
Kier Alexander as a temporary husband—but Kier has a proposition
of his own....

#2276 THE NIGHT OF THE WEDDING Kathryn Ross
Best friends become lovers, in this enjoyable read with a sexy
hero and sparky heroine! When Kate asked Nick to pretend to be
her escort at a wedding he reluctantly agreed. But to his surprise the
pretense came easily. And as night fell the mood deepened into
something neither he nor Kate had ever felt before....

HPCNM0802